THE LIFE OF KING DAVID

I Samuel 16 thru I Kings 2:12

by
Billy L Goe

authorHOUSE®

AuthorHouse™
1663 Liberty Drive, Suite 200
Bloomington, IN 47403
www.authorhouse.com
Phone: 1-800-839-8640

First published by AuthorHouse 8/20/2009

ISBN: 978-1-4343-5935-3 (sc)

Library of Congress Control Number: 2008902044

Printed in the United States of America
Bloomington, Indiana

This book is printed on acid-free paper.

The Lord said to Samuel the prophet, "How long will you mourn for Saul, seeing that I have rejected him from reigning over Israel? Fill your horn with oil, and go to Bethlehem, I will send you to Jesse: for I provided me a king among his sons." Samuel said, "How can I go?; if Saul hears about me going he will kill me." The Lord said, "Take an heifer with you and say, I am going to offer up a sacrifice to the Lord, and call Jesse to the sacrifice, and I will show you what you should do; and you anoint him unto Me, whom I will tell you." Samuel did as the Lord had told him. When he got to Bethlehem the elders of the town trembled because he was there, and they asked him, "Do you come in peace?" He answered, "Yes, I am come to offer up a sacrifice to the Lord: sanctify yourselves, and come with me to the sacrifice." Therefore Samuel sanctified Jesse and his sons, and invited them to the sacrifice. The name of Jesse's sons were: Eliab, Abinadab, Shimma, Nethaneel, Raddai, Ozem, and David. When all of Jesse's sons were gathered together, Samuel looked at Eliab and said, Surely the Lord's anointing is on you." The Lord said unto Samuel, "Do not look at his appearance or his height, because I have refused him: because the Lord does not see as men sees: man looks on the outward appearance, but the Lord looks at the heart." Therefore, Jesse made all of his sons gather together, and made each one of them stand in front of Samuel; as each one did he would say, "No, the Lord has not chosen this one." Then Jesse made each one of his sons stand before Samuel the second time, and, he said to Jesse, "The Lord has not chosen these." Samuel then asked Jesse, "Are these all of your children?" He said, "There is one more, the youngest, and he takes care of the sheep." Samuel said, "Go and get him, we will not sit down until he is here." So he did. David was ruddy, (reddish of the hair or the complexion) and a very good-looking young man. The Lord said, "Arise, and anoint him: for he is the one." Samuel took the horn of oil, and anointed David in front of all of his brothers, and the Spirit of the Lord was on David from that day on, but the Spirit of the Lord departed from Saul and an evil spirit from the Lord possessed him. Saul's servants said to him, "Tell us lord that stand before you to look for a man who is a talented harp player, so that when the evil spirit from God is on you, he will play his harp and you will be well. Saul said to his servants, "Find me a man that can play well and bring him to me, now.

One of the servants said, "I have seen one of Jesse's the Bethlehemite sons who is talented in playing, and a mighty brave man, a man of war, wise in matters a nice looking person and the Lord is with him. Saul sent messengers to Jesse and said, "Let me see David your son which is with the sheep. Jesse sent a donkey with a great variety of bread, a bottle of wine and a goat and gave them to David to give to Saul. He went to Saul and stood in front of him and, he loved him greatly. Saul made him his bodyguard. Therefore, Saul sent a message to Jesse saying, "Let David, I ask of you, stand with me, because he has found favor in my sight. When the evil spirit was on Saul, David would play his harp and the evil spirit would leave him and he would be well. The Philistines gathered together at Shochoh, which belonged to Judah, between Shodoh and Azekah, in Ephesdammin. Saul and the men of Israel were all together and camped by the valley of Elah, and set the battle in order to fight against the Philistines. All the Philistines stood on a mountain and, the Israelites stood on a mountain on the other side: there was a valley between them. Afterwards, out of the Philistine army came a great man of war named Goliath, of Gath who was thirteen feet and four inches tall. He had a helmet of brass on his head, he was armed with a coat of metal; and the weight of his coat was approx. 194.5 pounds. He had thongs around his calves and ankles made of brass and a shield of brass covering his chest. The handle of his sword was like a weaver's beam, and his sword's top weighed approx. 23 ½ pounds. It was made of iron, and there stood a man in front of him carrying a shield.

He stood and shouted at the armies of Israel and said, "Why are you come out to set your armies in order? Am I not a Philistine, and you servants of Saul's? Choose a man and, let him come and face me. If he is able to fight with me and kill me, then we will be your servants: but if I overtake him and kill him, then you will be our servants, and serve us." Then the Philistine said, "I will make the armies of Israel surrender today; let a man come down here so I can fight with him." When Saul and the Israelites heard what the Philistine had said, they were discouraged and very afraid. David was the son of Jesse an Ephrathite of Bethlehem-judah, which had eight sons. He lived in Israel all of his life. His three oldest sons followed Saul to the battle and, their names were Eliab, Abinadab, and Shammah, and David was the youngest. While the three oldest sons followed Saul, David went back to Bethlehem to feed his father's sheep, while the Philistine drew closer morning and evening and was in battle for forty days. Jesse told David, his son, "Take this one bushel of parched wheat, ten loaves of bread and run to the camp to your brothers, and take these ten cheeses to the captain of the ten-thousand soldiers and look and see how your brothers are doing and tell each of them to give you something to let me know that they are alive and well, and bring it back to me. Now Saul, Jesse's sons and all the men of Israel were in the valley of Elah fighting with the Philistines. David got up early the next morning and left the sheep with a keeper and went to do what his father had told him, as he came to the trench the soldiers were going to battle and, they shouted. The Israelites and the Philistines put the battle in order, army against army. David left his things with someone, and ran into the army and found his brothers, and as he was talking to them, Goliath the Philistine said again, "Why did you go out and set your armies in order? Am I not a Philistine, and you the servants of Saul? Choose a man, and, let him come and fight with me." David heard him, and when the Israelites saw Goliath they all ran away and were very afraid.

The men of Israel said, "Have you seen this man? Surely he will destroy Israel. If any man can kill Goliath, the king will give him all kinds of riches, and he will get to marry his daughter, and everyone in his father's home will not have to be in the military court nor any other services."

David said to the men that stood by him, "What will happen to the man that kills this Philistine and takes away the shame from Israel? For who is this uncircumcised Philistine, that he would destroy the armies of the living God?" Therefore, the people answered his question saying, "This will happen to the man that kills this Philistine."

Eliab, David's oldest brother heard what he said to the men, and he was very angry at David and said, "Why did you come down here? Who have you left the few sheep in the wilderness with? I know your pride and the naughtiness of your heart. You have come down here hoping that you could see the battle." David said, "What have I done now? Isn't there a good reason for me to be asking these questions?"

He turned away from his brother and started talking to someone else and asking the same questions. Afterwards they went and told Saul what he had said and, Saul wanted to see David.

David said to Saul, "Let no man fear because of him. I your servant will go and fight this Philistine." Saul said, "You are not able to fight against Goliath. You are just a boy and he is a man of war from his boyhood." David answered him and said, "Your servant kept his father's sheep, and a lion came, and a bear and took a lamb out of the flock, and I went after him and attacked him and took the lamb out of his mouth: and when he stood up to fight against me, I grabbed him by his beard and attacked him, and killed him. I killed the lion and the bear, and this uncircumcised Philistine will be like one of them seeing he has mocked the armies of the living God. Seeing that the Lord had delivered me from being killed by the lion and the bear, He will also keep me from being killed by this Philistine." Saul said, "Go, and may the Lord be with you."

Saul then put his armor on David, and a helmet of bronze on his head and a coat of metal around his chest, and David strapped his sword on his armor and he began to go, because he had not tried it out. He said to Saul, "I cannot use this armor, because I am not use to it." David took the armor off.

He took his staff and picked up five smooth stones out of the water, and put them in his shepherd's bag and, a scrip, and, his sling was in his hand, and David and the Philistine began walking toward each other and the man that packed the shield was in front of Philistine.

When the Philistine looked around and saw David he despised him: for he was just a boy and ruddy (reddish of the hair or the complexion) and was very good-looking. The Philistine said to David, "Am I a dog that you would come at me with staves?" They cursed David by their gods, then Philistine said, "Come here to me and, I will give your flesh to the birds of the air, and to the animals of the field." David said to the Philistine, "You come to me with a sword, spear and a shield, but I come to you in the name of the Lord of Host, the God of the armies of Israel, who you have mocked. Today the Lord will deliver you into my hand and, I will kill you and cut your head off and, I will give your body to the birds of the air and to the wild animals of the earth, so that all the people of the world may know that there is a God in Israel, then all the people will know that the Lord does not save with a sword and spear: for the battle is the Lord's, and He will put you in our hands.

The Philistine stood up and ran toward David, then he ran toward the army to meet the Philistine. He put his hand in his bag, and took out a stone and slung it, and hit the Philistine on the forehead: and he fell to the ground face first. David ran and stood on top of the Philistine and took his sword and drew it out of the sheath and cut off the Philistine's head, and when they saw there champion was dead they ran away. David defeated the Philistine with a sling and a stone and hit and killed him, but there was no sword in David's hand.

The men of Israel and of Judah stood up and shouted and chased after the Philistines until they came to the valley, and to the gates of Ekron, and the wounded Philistines fell down on the way to Shaaraim, Gath and Ekron.

The children of Israel returned from chasing after the Philistines, and they took their goods out of their tents. David took the head of the Philistine to Jerusalem and put his armor in his tent.

When Saul seen David fight the Philistine, he said to Abner, the captain of the army, "Who is this boy's father?" Abner said, "As long as your soul lives, O king, I cannot tell." The king said, "Find out whose son his boy is."

Therefore when David returned from killing the Philistine, Abner grabbed him and took him to Saul with the head of the Philistine in his hand: and Saul said to him, "Whose son are you young man?" David said, "I am the servant of your servant Jesse, the Bethlehemite.

Afterwards when David had finished talking with Saul, Jonathan respected and loved David very much. Saul wouldn't let David return to his father's home no more.

Jonathan and David made a covenant together, because he loved him very much. He took off his clothes and gave them to David even his sword, his bow and his girdle.

David went everywhere Saul told him, and he acted very grown-up: and Saul made him ruler over the men of war, and he was respected by all of the people and also of Saul's servants.

Afterwards, when David returned from killing the Philistine, the women came out of all the cities of Israel, singing and dancing, to meet king Saul, playing tabrets with joy, and with instruments of music. The women said to one another as they played, "Saul has killed thousands, and David has killed tens of thousands." Saul was very angry, and he didn't like what the women were saying about him and he said, "They have said that David had killed tens of thousand but that I've killed thousands. I am the king, not David. Saul watched David with suspicion from that day on.

The next day the evil spirit from God came upon Saul, and he prophesied in front of the people: and David played with his hand, as he had done before: and there was a javelin in Saul's hand, and he threw the javelin at the wall, and, David escaped twice from being hit.

Saul was afraid of David, because he knew the Lord was with David, and not with him. Therefore Saul wasn't around David, but he made him his captain over a thousand men, and he went in and out before the people. David acted very mature in every way, and the Lord was with him. Wherefore when Saul noticed how he was acting he was afraid of him, but everyone in Israel and Judah loved David, because he went around them.

Saul said to David, "Here is my oldest daughter Merab, I will let you two get married, all you have to do is be valiant for me, and fight the Lord's battles. Saul thought to himself, I will not kill David I will let the Philistines kill him. David said, "Who am I? What is my life, or my father's family in Israel, that I should be a son-in-law to the king? When it was time for them to get married, she married Adriel the Meholathite instead of David, but Michal, Saul's daughter loved David: and they told Saul and he was all for it. He said, " I will let them get married, so she can be a snare to him, so the Philistines will be against him. Wherefore Saul said to David, "You will be my son-in-law when you marry one of my daughters."

Saul told his servants, "Talk to David secretly, and say, the king is pleased with you, and all of his servants love you: you should be the king's son-in-law." Saul's servant did what they were told. David said, "You all act like it's a small thing to be the king's son-in-law. I am a poor and a very young man." Saul's servants went and told him what David has said. He told his servants to go and tell David, "The king does not want any money, but a hundred foreskins of the Philistines, to be taken from the king's enemies. He thought that the Philistines would kill David.

When Saul's servants went and told David what the king had said, it made him very happy to be the king's son-in-law: but it wasn't time for David and Michal to get married yet.

Wherefore David went, he and his men, and killed two-hundred Philistines; and David brought their foreskins and gave them all to the king, that he might be the king's son-in-law. Saul let Michal, his daughter, marry David. He knew the Lord was with David and that his daughter loved him. Therefore, Saul was even more afraid of him: and he became David's enemy from there on. Afterwards, when the princes of the Philistines came around, and David acted more mature than all the servants of Saul; he was very well thought of.

Saul spoke to Jonathan and all his servants about killing David, but Jonathan thought a lot of him. Jonathan told David, "My dad wants to kill you so watch out for yourself until morning, and hide where no one will find you. I will go out and stand beside my dad in the field where you are, and I will talk to him about you and whatever I see I will tell you." He only said good things about David to his dad, Jonathan said to his dad, "Don't let the king sin against his servant, David: because he has not sinned against you, because he has only done good things for you. He did put his life into his own hands by slaying Goliath, and, the Lord gave a great victory to all of Israel: you saw it and rejoiced, so then why are you wanting to shed innocent blood by killing him? He's never giving you a reason to!" Saul listened to what his son had to say, and he swore, "As the Lord lives, David will not be killed." Jonathan went and told David everything he and his dad had said, and he brought David to Saul, and he was around him like before.

When another war broke out, David went out and fought and killed many of the Philistines, and they ran from him. The evil spirit from the Lord was upon Saul, when he was in his house with his javelin in his hand: and David played music on his harp. He tried to kill David with the javelin; but he ran off and Saul hit the wall instead. David fled and escaped that night. Saul sent messengers to David's house, to watch him, and to kill him in the morning: then Michal, David's wife told him, "If you don't protect your self tonight, you will be dead in the morning!" She helped David get out through a window and he fled and escaped. Michal took an household image, and laid it in the bed, and put a pillow of goats' hair for his body, and covered it with a blanket, when Saul sent messengers to kill David, Michal said that he was sick, then Saul sent the messengers again to see David, and told them to tell Michal, "Bring David to me in the bed, so I can kill him." When the messengers returned to David's house all they found was an image in the bed, with a pillow of goats' hair for his body.

Saul said to Michal, "why have you deceived me like this, and let my enemy escape, and she answered him, "He said to me, Let me go; why should I kill you?"

David fled, and escaped, and went to where Samuel was in Ramah, and told him everything that Saul had done to him, and they went and stayed in Naioth.

Someone told Saul, that David is at Naioth in Ramah; therefore Saul sent messengers to bring David to him: and when they saw the prophets prophesying, and Samuel standing as appointed over them, the Spirit of God was upon the messengers of Saul, and they also prophesied. Saul was told about this, and he sent other messengers, and they also prophesied like the ones before, so he sent even more messengers the third time and they also prophesied. Saul, himself went to Ramah, and came to a great well that is in Sechu: and he asked someone, "Where are Samuel and David?" They answered him, "They are in Naioth in Ramah." He went to Naoith in Ramah: and the Spirit of God was upon him also, and he prophesied, until he came to Naioth in Ramah. He stripped off his clothes also, and prophesied in front of Samuel like his messengers did, and lay down naked all day and all night. Therefore everyone was saying, "Is Saul also among the prophets?"

David left Naioth in Ramah, and went and told Jonathan, "What have I done?" "What sin have I committed?" "What sin have I committed against your dad?" "Why does he want to kill me?" Jonathan said, "God forbid!: you will not die. My dad will not do anything without telling me first. Why would he hide it from me? Do you think I'm right?" David said, "Your dad certainly knows that you are a good friend of mine. He thinks, I will not let Jonathan know what I'm going to do so he won't grieve, but just as sure as the Lord lives and your soul lives, there is but one step between David and death." Jonathan said, "What ever you want or need I will do it for you." David said, "Tomorrow is the new moon, and I should sit with the king at dinner, but I will go and hide in the field until the third day at evening. If your dad misses me, then tell him, that I went to Beth-lehem where I'm from: for there is a yearly sacrifice there for all the family. If he says that it's alright: my servant shall have peace: but if he gets angry, then know that he is going to do something evil! Therefore you shall deal nicely with your servant: for you have brought him into a covenant of the Lord with you: but, if there be in me iniquity, kill me yourself; for why should you bring me to your father?" Jonathan said, "Let it be far from you: for if I know for sure that my dad was going to harm you in any way, wouldn't I tell you?" David said, "Who is going to tell me? Or what if your dad is angry with you?" Jonathan said, "Let's go out into the field," so they went out into the field. Jonathan said, "O Lord, the God of Israel, be my witness, when I know what my father is going to do tomorrow or any other time, if he isn't going to do anything bad to you, and I don't find you and tell you, the Lord do the evil and much more than that to me, but if my dad is going to harm you in any way, then I will tell you, and send you away that you may go in peace, and may the Lord be with you as he has been with my dad. As long as I live you shall show me the kindness of the Lord, so I won't die, but after I'm dead, you will show my family your kindness forever: no, not even when the Lord has taken away all of your enemies.

Therefore, Jonathan made a covenant with the family of David, saying, "Let the Lord require it at the hand of David's enemies. He also made David to vow again, because he loved him: for he loved him as he loved his own soul. Jonathan said to David, "Tomorrow is the new moon: and you will be missed, because you will not be there; but, when you have been gone three days, then you will come down quickly, and come to the place where you hide yourself when the business was Happening, and then you need to remain by the stone Ezel. I will shoot three arrows on the side, as though I shot at a mark. I will send a young man and tell him, go and find the arrows. If I expressly say to him, the arrows are on this side of you, take them; then come out: for there is peace to you, and no harm, as the Lord lives, but if I say to the young man, behold, the arrows are beyond you; go your way: for the Lord has sent you away; what we were talking about earlier, behold the Lord be between you and me forever."

Therefore, David hid himself in the field: and when the new moon was come, the king sat down to eat meat, when he sat down in his seat, as he did at other times, on the seat by the wall, Jonathan stood up, and Abner sat by Saul's side, and David's place way empty. Nevertheless Saul didn't say anything that day: for he thought something had happened to David, he is not clean: surely he is unclean.

The next day, which was the second day of the month, David's place was empty: and Saul said to Jonathan his son, "Why is Jesse's son not at dinner, neither yesterday nor today?" Jonathan answered, "David earnestly asked leave so he could go to Beth-lehem. He said to me, Let me go, I ask of you; for our family has a sacrifice in the city; and my brother, he has commanded me to be there: and now, if I have found favor in your eyes let me go away and see my brothers. That is why he is not at the king's table."

Saul was not angry with Jonathan, then he said to him, "Son of the perverse rebellious woman, don't you think I know that you have chosen the son of Jesse to your own shame, and to the shame of your mother's nakedness? For as long as the son of Jesse lives, you will not be established, nor your kingdom. Now go get him and bring him to me for he shall surely die!" Jonathan said, "Why shall he be killed? What has he done?" Saul threw a javelin at him to hit him: then Jonathan knew that his father was determined to kill David. He got up from the table in fierce anger, and didn't eat because he was grieved for David, because his father had done him shame.

The next morning Jonathan went out into the field at the time he told David he would be there with a young man with him. He said to the young man, "Run, find the arrows that I will shoot." as the young man ran, he shot an arrow beyond him. When the young man got to the place of the arrow which Jonathan had shot, he shouted at the lad, and said, "Is not the arrow beyond you? Hurry up! Do not delay!" The young man gathered up the arrows and came back to Jonathan, but he knew nothing, only Jonathan and David know what was going on. Jonathan gave his artillery to the young man, and said, "Go, take them to the city." When the young man was gone, David arose and fell on his face to the ground, and bowed three times: and they kissed one another, and wept. Jonathan said to David, "Go in peace, just as we have vowed, both of us in the name of the Lord, saying, The Lord be between me and you, and between my seed and your seed for ever;" and he arose and left: and Jonathan went into the city.

David went to Nob to see Ahimelech the priest: and Ahimelech was afraid when he saw him and said, "Why are your alone?" David said to him, "The king has giving me something to do, and said to me, do not let anyone know about what I have commanded of you, and I have told my servants to be at such and such a place. Now what do you have on hand? Give me five loaves of bread and whatever you have." The priest said to David, "I have no ordinary bread, but there is hallowed (holy) bread: if the young men have at least not been with any women." David said, "I have not been around any women in about three days, since I came out, and that's the truth. The vessels of the young men are holy, and the bread is technically common, yea though I were consecrated today in the vessel." Therefore, the priest gave him the hallowed bread that was taken before the Lord.

One of Saul's servants was there that day, detained before the Lord; and his name was Doeg, an Edomite the chief of Saul's shepherds. David said to Ahimelech, "Don't you have a spear or a sword?" I didn't bring my sword or any of my weapons with me, because I had to hurry and do what the king wanted me to do." The priest said, "The sword of Goliath the Philistine, whom you killed in the valley of Elah is here wrapped in a cloth behind the ephod: if you want to take it, take it, that is the only one here." David said, "There is no other sword like that one, give it to me." David left that day because he feared Saul, and went to Achish the king of Gath. The servants of Achish said to him, "Is not this David the king of the land? Didn't all the people sing of him and danced, saying Saul has killed thousands but David has killed ten of thousands?" David took these words to heart, and was very afraid of Achish. He changed the way he acted around them and acted insane , and scratched on the doors of the gate, and let spittle run down into his beard. Achish said to his servants, "You see that this man is insane: so why have you brought him to me? "Do I have a need a mad man; is that why you brought him to me? Shall this man come into my house?"

David left and went to the cave Adullam: and when his dad and brothers heard where he was they went to see him. Everyone that was in distress, every one that was in debt, and every one that was grieved went to him and he became a captain over them: and there were about four hundred men there.

David left there and went to Mizpeh of Moab: and he said to the king of Moab, "Let my dad and my mom, come here and stay with you until I know what God wants me do to." Therefore, he brought them to the king of Moab: and they lived there with him while David was in the stronghold. The prophet Gad told David, "Do not stay in the stronghold: leave and go to the land of Judah." David left, and went to the forest of Hareth.

When Saul heard where David was, and the men that were with him (now Saul was in Gibeah under a tree in Ramah with his spear in his hand, and all his servants were standing there with him.) He said to his servants, "Listen to me, you Benjamites: will Jesse's son give every one of you fields and vineyards, and make you all captains of thousands, and captains of hundreds?"

All of you have plotted against me, and none of you has shown me that my son has made a covenant with Jesse's son, and none of you feel sorry for me or has shown me that my son has made my servant angry with me, and is probably lying in wait for me somewhere."

Then Doeg the Edomite, which was theruler over the servants of Saul said, "I saw Jesse's son going to Nob, to Ahimelech the son of Ahitub. He prayed to the Lord for him and gave him food, and the sword of Goliah the Philistine." The king sent for Ahimelech the priest, Ahitub's son and everyone that was in his house, and all the priests of Nob: and all of them came to Saul. Then he said, "Listen to me Ahitub's son, and he answered him, "Here I am, my lord." Saul said to him, "Why are you and David against me? Why did you give him bread, and a sword, and prayed to God for him, that he should come against me?" Ahimelech answered the king, and said, "Who of all your servants is as faithful as David, which is your son-in-law, and goes when you tell him to, and who is honorable? Did I then pray to God for him? Don't even think that I did. Do not accuse me of this, nor to anyone in my family: for your servant knew nothing of this at all, no less or no more." The king said, "You shall surely die, Ahimelech, you and everyone in your father's house." He said to his guards that stood around him, "Turn, and kill the priests of the Lord; because they are also on David's side, and because they knew when David ran away and did not tell me." The guards of the king would not as much as put their hands on the priests of the Lord to kill them. The king said to Doeg, "Turn, and attack the priests." Therefore Doeg turned, and attacked the priests, and killed eighty-five priests that day.

Doeg killed every man, woman, child, baby, ox, donkey, and sheep with his sword in Nob, the city of the priest. One of the sons of Ahimelech the son of Ahitub, named Abiathar, escaped, and went after David. He showed David that Saul had killed the Lord's priests. David said to him, "I know when he killed them, when Doeg was there, I know that he would tell Saul: I have caused the death of all the people of your family. Stay here with me, and don't be afraid: because he that wants to kill me wants to kill you too: but with me you will be safe."

Abiathar then told David, "Look, the Philistines are fighting against Keilah, and they are robbing the threshing floors." David then asked of the Lord, "Shall go and kill the Philistines?"

The Lord said, "Go, and kill the Philistines, and save Keilah." David's men said to him, "We are afraid here in Judah: and we are more afraid to go to Keilah and fight against the armies of the Philistines." David asked the Lord again, and the Lord told him, "Get up and go to Keilah; because I will deliver the Philistines into your hand." David and his men went to Keilah, and fought with the Philistines, and took their cattle, and killed them with a great slaughter. David saved the people of Keilah.

Afterwards, when Abiathar found David in Keilah, he had an ephod in his hand. Saul was told that David was there. Saul said, "God has delivered him into my hand; for he is shut in, by entering into a town that is surrounded by gates and bars." He called all the people of war together to war, to go down to Keilah, and surround David and his men. David knew that Saul secretly was out to harm him; and he said to Abiathar the priest, "Bring me the ephod." David then prayed to the Lord, "O Lord God of Israel, your servant has certainly heard that Saul seeks to come to Keilah, to destroy the city because of me. Will the men of Keilah deliver me up into his hand? Will Saul come to Keilah as I have heard? O Lord God of Israel, I beg you tell me." The Lord said, "He will come down to Keilah." David said, "Will the men of Keilah deliver me and my men into the hand of Saul?" The Lord said, "They will deliver you out of Saul's hand." David and his men, about six hundred, left there, and went where ever they could go. Someone told Saul that David had escaped, and he forbid to go and look for him. David stayed in the wilderness in strongholds, and remained in a mountain in the wilderness of Ziph. Saul sought him every day, but God delivered him not into his hand. David knew that Saul was out to kill him, so he was in the wilderness of Ziph in Horesh. Jonathan went and found David, and strengthened his faith in God. He said, "Do not be afraid: because my dad will not find you; you shall be king of Israel, and I shall be next in rank below you, and my dad knows this." They made a covenant before the Lord: and David stayed in Horesh and Jonathan went home.

Afterwards the Ziphites came to Saul at Gibeah, and said, "Isn't David hiding with us in strongholds in the woods, in the hills of Hachilah, which is south of Jeshimon? Now therefore king come down here like you want to and we shall try to deliver him into your hand." Saul said, "May the Lord bless you, for you have had compassion on me. Go I ask of you and prepare and find out where he is hiding, and who has seen him. I was told that he is very cunningly. See where he is lurking and where he is hiding, and come back here and tell me, and I will go back there with you, and I will search for him throughout all the people of Judah." They went to Ziph before Saul: but David and his men were in the wilderness of Maon, in the plain south of Jeshimon. Saul and his men went to find him, and they told David: therefore he went down to a rock and stayed there in the wilderness of Maon. When Saul heard about it, he looked for David in the wilderness of Maon. He went on one side of the mountain, and David and his men on the other side. David hurried to get away because he feared Saul; because Saul and his men surrounded him and his men in order to kill them. There was a messenger that came to Saul and said, "Hurry! For the Philistines have invaded the land." Therefore Saul returned home and quit looking for David, and therefore they called that place Sela-hammablekoth (translated Rock of Escaping). David went from there and stayed in strongholds at En-gedi.

When Saul returned from pursuing the Philistines, someone said to him, "David is in the wilderness of En-gedi." He and three thousand chosen men in all of Israel, went to find David and his men upon the rocks of the wild goats. He came to the sheepfolds on the way, to a cave and Saul went in to attend to his needs: and David and his men stayed in the sides of the cave. David's men said to him, "The day in which the Lord said to you, I will deliver your enemy into your hands, that you may do to him what you think is right." Therefore he got up and cut off the skirt of Saul's robe privately. David was very bothered because he had done this. He said to his men, "The Lord forbid that I should do this thing to my master, the Lord's anointed, to stretch forth my hand against him, seeing he is the anointed of the Lord." He restrained his servants with these words, and did not allow them to go against Saul. Saul went out of the cave and went his way. David also left the cave, and went after him, saying, "My lord the king." When Saul looked behind him, David stopped and looked down on the ground and bowed down, and said to, "Did you hear my men say that I seek to kill thee? Today I have seen how that the Lord had delivered you today into my hand in the cave, and some wanted me to kill you: but my eyes spared you; and I said, I will not try to hurt my lord, for he is the Lord's anointed. My dad saw the corner of your robe in my hand: because I cut it off of your robe, and I didn't kill you. See there is neither evil nor rebellion in my heard, and I have not sinned against you; yet you are hunting me down to kill me. May the Lord judge both you and me, and may He avenge me of you: but I will not try to harm you. Just as the proverb of the ancients, Wickedness proceeds from the wicked: but my hand shall not harm you. Who is the king of Israel after? Who are you looking for? A dead dog, a flea?"

When David had finished talking to Saul, Saul said, "Is this your voice, my son David?" Hel wept and said to David, "You are more righteous than me: for you have rewarded me good, whereas I rewarded you evil. You have showed me today that you have dealt well with me: because when the Lord had delivered me into your hands, you did not kill me. If a man catch his enemy will he let him go his way? May the Lord reward you good for that you have done for me today. Now I know that you will be king, and that the kingdom of Israel shall be established in your hand. Swear now to me by the Lord, that you will not cut off my seed after me, and that you will not destroy my name in my dad's house." David swore to Saul, and he went home; but David and his men went into the stronghold.

When Samuel died; all the Israelites gathered together to grieve over him, and they buried him in his hometown of Ramah. David went down to the wilderness of Paran.

There was a man in Maon, who owned a business in Carmel; and the man was very wealthy, he had three-thousand sheep, and a thousand goats: and he was shearing his sheep in Carmel. The man's name was Nabal, and his wife's name was Abigail, she was very intelligent and beautiful: but Nabal was harsh and evil; his dad was Caleb. While David was in the wilderness, he had heard that Nabal was shearing his sheep. He sent ten of his young men to Nabal and said to them, "Go to Carmel and greet him in my name. Peace be to you and your family and to all that you own. I have heard that you have shearers. Your shepherds which were with us, we did not hurt them, neither was there anything they had missing, all the time we were in Carmel. Ask your young men, and they will show you. Therefore be gracious unto the young men and let them find favor in your eyes: for we come in a good day: give, I ask of you, whatsoever you have, give it to your servants, and to your son David." So when the young men went to Nabal, they told him exactly what David had said. Nabal answered David's servants, "Who is David? Who is the son of Jesse? There are many servants nowadays that run away from their master. Shall I take my bread, water, and my meat that I have killed for my shearers, and give it other men, who I do not know? Therefore David's men went back to him and told him everything that Nabal had said. David said to his men, "Everyone put your sword on your side." David also put his sword on his side: and there went up with David about four-hundred men; and two-hundred stayed there with the baggage.

One of the young men told Abigail, Nabal's wife, "David sent messengers out of the wilderness to greet our master; and he scolded them. The men were very good to us, and we were not hurt, neither did we miss anything, as long as we accompanied them in the fields: They surrounded us both day and night, while we were tending to the sheep. We want you to know this, so you can determine what you will do, because something bad is going to happen to our master, and all of his family: for he is such a wicked man, that no one can speak to him."

Abigail went away quickly, and took two hundred loaves of bread, two bottles of wine, five sheep ready dressed, five measures of roasted grain, a hundred clusters of raisins, and two hundred cakes of figs, and laid them on donkeys. She told her servants, "Go to where David is, I will be there shortly." She did not tell her husband Nabal. When she was going down by the covert of the hill, David and his men was going to attack her, and she met them. David said, "Surely in vain I have taken all that Nabal had in the wilderness, so that nothing was missing of all he had; and he has done good to me for the evil that did to him. May God do more than this to my enemies, if I leave everything that I took from him to any man that finds it."

When Abigail saw David, she got off the donkey and bowed down to the ground before him, and fell at his feet, and said, "My lord, let this iniquity be on me: and let your handmaid, I ask of you, speak in the company of your servants, and hear what I have to say. Do not let my lord, I ask of you, regard this evil man, Nabal. Nabal, for as his name is, so is he; (foolish, wicked) Nabal is his name, and he does foolish things, but me your handmaid did not see the young men of my lord, whom you did send. Now therefore, my lord, as the Lord lives, and as your soul lives, seeing the Lord has not allowed you to kill me, and delivering yourself, now let your enemies, and they that want to kill you, be as Nabal. This gift which your handmaiden has brought you, let it also be given to the young men that are with you. I ask of you, forgive me of the sin that I have done: because the Lord will certainly make your house an enduring one, because you fight the battles of the Lord and you have never done anything evil. Yet has a man risen up to find you and kill you: but the life of my lord shall live with the Lord God; and the souls of your enemies, them shall the Lord sling out, as out of a hollow of a sling, and It shall happen, when the Lord has done to you all the good things that He has spoken concerning you, and shall appoint you ruler over Israel. This shall not be something that troubles you, nor something that you'll be sorry you did, because you have not shed innocent blood without cause, or because you have delivered yourself: but when the Lord shall deal with you, then remember me." David said to Abigail, "Blessed be the Lord God of Israel, which sent you today to meet me: and blessed be your advice and may you be blessed, because you have kept me from killing an innocent person, and from delivering myself. As the Lord God of Israel lives, He has kept me from hurting you, if you had not came quickly to meet me, surely there would have been no men of Nabal's in the morning."

David took what she had brought to him, and said to her, "Go back to your house in peace: because I have listened to you, and I believe you."

Therefore, Abigail went to Nabal; and he had a very large feast, like the feast of a king; and he was very happy because he was very drunk: therefore she told him nothing that has happened, until the next morning, when he had sobered up then his wife told him everything that has happened, then Nabal had a stroke. Approximately ten days later the Lord struck Nabal and he died.

When David heard that Nabal was dead, he said, "Blessed be the Lord, who has pleaded the cause of my disgrace with Nabal, and has kept His servant from evil: for the Lord has returned the wickedness of Nabal to him." He sent servants to Abigail, to ask her to marry him. And when his servants of got to Abigail in Carmel, they said to her, "David sent us to you to ask you to be his wife." She stood up and bowed her face to the ground, "Let me be a servant and wash the feet of the servants of my lord." She arose quickly, and rode a donkey, with five damsels of hers that went with her; and she went with the messengers of David, and became his wife. David also took Ahinoam of Jezreel; and they were both his wives. But Saul had given Michal his daughter, David's wife, to Phalti the son of Laish, which was of Gallim.

The Ziphites came to Saul to Gibeah, and said, "Isn't David hiding on the hill of Hachilah, which is right before Jeshimon?" Saul stood up and went down to the wilderness of Ziph, bringing three thousand chosen men of Israel with him, to find David in the wilderness of Ziph.

He camped in the hill of Hachilah, which is before Jeshimon, but David stayed in the wilderness, he knew that Saul was after him in the wilderness. He therefore sent out spies, to make sure that Saul was also in the wilderness. He stood up, and went to the place where Saul had camped; and saw the place where Saul had lain, and Abner, the captain of his host; and Saul lay in the tent, and the people camped around him. David said to Ahimelech, and to Abishai, "Who will go with me to where Saul is camping?" Abishai answered, "I will go with you."

That night David and Abishai went to where the people were, and Saul lay sleeping in the camp and his spear was stuck in the ground at his head: but Abner and the people lay all around him. Abishai said to David, "God has delivered your enemy into your hand: now therefore let me hit him, I ask to of you, with the spear one time, and I will not hit him again." David answered Abishai, "Do not destroy him: for who can stretch forth his hand against the Lord's anointed and be found innocent?" Then he said, "As the Lord lives, the Lord shall kill him; or he will die someday; or he shall go down to battle and die. The Lord will not let me kill His anointed; but, I ask of you take his spear that is at his head, and the cruse of water, and let's get out of here. David took the spear and the cruse of water from Saul's head and they went away, and no one saw them or knew they were there, for they were all asleep; because the Lord made a deep sleep fall on them.

David went over to the other side of the mountain, and stood on the top of a hill far away; a great distance from Saul: He cried to the people, and to Abner saying, "Aren't you going to answer, Abner?" He then answered and said, "Who is it that cries to the king?" David said to Abner, "Aren't you a man? Who is like you in Israel? Why then have your not guarded your lord the king? Someone came in to destroy the him. This is not good what you have done. As the Lord lives, you are worthy of death, because you have not guarded your master, the Lord's anointed; and now see where the king's spear is, and the cruse of water that was at his head?"

Saul recognized David's voice and knew that it was him, and said, "Is that you, my son David?" David said, "It is me my lord, O king." Then he said, "Why are you looking for your servant, my lord? What have I done, or what evil thing have I done? Now therefore, I beg of you let my lord the king hear my words. If the Lord has made you mad at me; let Him accept an offering: but if someone else has made you mad at me, may they be cursed before the Lord; for they have run me out from living in the inheritance of the Lord, and said, Go, serve other gods; now therefore, do not kill me before the Lord, for the king of Israel is come out to look for a flea, as when one hunts a partridge in the mountains."

Saul said, "I have sinned: go on home, my son: for I will do no more harm to you, because my soul was precious to you: I have been a fool, and have made a terrible mistake." David answered and said, "Look, the king's spear! Let one of the young men take it. May the Lord reward every man his according to his righteousness and faithfulness: for the Lord delivered you into my hand today, but I would not do my Lord's anointed any harm, because your life held great value to me so let my life be of great value in the eyes of the Lord, and let him deliver me out of all tribulation." Saul said, "You are blessed, my son David: you shall do great things and you shall prevail." Afterwards David went his way, and Saul returned to his house.

David said in his heart, "Saul will one day kill me: the best thing I can do is to go to Philistine quickly; and he shall get tired of looking for me in Israel: so he shall do me no harm."

Therefore, he arose, he and 600 men that were with him, and went to Achish, king of Gath. He lived with Achish at Gath, he and his men, including his two wives, Ahinoam the Jezreelitess, and Abigail the Carmelitess, Nabal's wife. Someone went and told Saul that David had went to Gath: but he didn't go after him anymore. David said to Achish, "If I have found favor in your eyes, let your people give me a place to live in some town in the country, for why should your servant live in the royal city with you?" Achish gave him Ziklag that day: (Ziklag pertains to the kings of Judah until this day.) He lived in Ziklag one year and four months.

David and his men went and attacked the Geshurites, the Gezrites, and the Amalekites: (enemies of Israel Joshua had not defeated) because the people that lived there were there since ancient times. The land was from Shur, even unto the land of Egypt. David attacked the land and left not a man or woman alive, and took all the sheep, and the oxen, and the asses, and the camels, and the apparel, and went to Achish, and he said to David, "Where have you raided today?" David said, "Against the south of Judah, and against the south of the Jerahmeelites, and against the south of the Kenites." He killed all the men and all the women, so he could take everything they owned to Gath, so they wouldn't be saying, "David took everything we own, and he will keep on doing this as long as he lives in the country of the Philistines."

Achish believed David, and said, "He has made his people Israel completely to disapprove of him; therefore he shall be my servant forever."

One day the Philistines gathered their armies together for war, to fight against Israel. Achish said to David, "You do know that you and your men will go to fight against Israel with me?" David said, "Surely you will know what your servant can do." He answered and said, "Therefore I will make you one of my chief guardians forever!"

Samuel was dead, and all of Israel had mourned because of his death, and buried him in Ramah, the city where he was born. Saul sent away those that had familiar spirits, the mediums and the spiritists and the wizards, out of the land.

The Philistines gathered together in Shunem and camped there: and Saul got Israel together, and they camped in Gilboa. When Saul seen all the armies of the Philistines, he was afraid, and his heart greatly trembled. Saul prayed to the Lord, the Lord did not answer him.

Saul then said to his servants, "Find me a woman that is a medium, (someone who can transmit messages between the living and the dead.) that I can go to her, and ask her what I should do." His servants said, "There is a woman that is a medium at En-dor." The woman said to Saul, "Look, you know what you have done, how you have cut off those that have familiar spirits, and the wizards, out of the land: why then are you laying a snare for my life, to cause me to die? Saul swore to her by the Lord, saying, "As the Lord lives, you will receive no punishment for this thing." The woman said, "Who do you want me to bring up for you?" He said, "Bring up Samuel." When the woman saw Samuel, she cried with a loud voice: and said to Saul, "Why have you deceived me? You are Saul!" He said, "Do not be afraid: what did you see?" The woman said, I saw spirits ascending out of the earth." Saul said, "What did he look like?" She said, "An old man came up; and he was covered with a mantle." Saul thought that it was Samuel, and he stooped down with his face to the ground, and bowed down. Samuel said to Saul, "Why have you disturbed me and brought me up?" Saul answered, "I am deeply distressed; the Philistines want to go to war against me, and God has departed from me, and will not answer me in any way, therefore I have called you so you can tell me what I should do." Samuel said, "Why then do you ask me, knowing that the Lord has departed from you, and has become your enemy? The Lord has done to David what He told me He would do. The Lord has taken away from you your kingdom and has given it to David, because you would not obey Him nor did you execute His fierce judgment on Amalek, that is why to Lord has done this to you. The Lord will also deliver Israel with you into the hands of the Philistines: and tomorrow you and your sons will be with me: the Lord also will deliver the Israelites from the Philistines." Saul fell to the ground, and was very afraid, because of what Samuel has said to him. He had no strength because he had not eaten all day nor all night. The woman came to Saul and saw that he was severely troubled, and said to him, "I have done everything you have asked of me, and I have put my life in my own hands, and have listened to every word you've said, now I ask of you, let me make you something to eat, so that you will have strength when you leave." He refused and said, "I will not eat." All of his servants and the woman urged him: and he listened to them. He got up off the ground, and sat on the bed. The woman had a fat calf and she quickly killed it, and took flour, and kneaded it, and baked unleavened bread, and brought it to Saul, and his servants and they ate, and then that night they left.

The Philistines gathered all their armies together at Aphek: and the Israelites encamped by a fountain at Jezreel. The lords of the Philistines went to war by hundreds, and by thousands: but David and his men went in the back way with Achish.

The princes of the Philistines said, "What are these Hebrews doing here"? Achish said to the princes of the Philistines, "Is this not David, the servant of Saul the king of Israel, which has been with me for the last year and four months, and I know of nothing this man has done wrong the entire time he's been with me?" The princes of the Philistines were angry with him; and they said to him, "Make this man return, that he may go back to where you appointed him, and do not let him go down with us into battle, so there's no chance he will be an enemy to us: how will he reconcile with his master? It should be with the heads of these men. Is this not David, of whom they sang and danced about saying, Saul killed thousands, and David ten thousand?"

Achish called David, and said to him, "Surely, as the Lord lives, you have done nothing wrong and you've done nothing wrong while you were with my army. I have seen you do no evil since you've been with me, nevertheless the lords do not like you, therefore I want you to return, and go in peace, so you do not upset the lords of the Philistines." David said, "What have I done?" "What have you seen me do that was so wrong, that you don't want me to go fight against the enemies of my lord the king? Achish answered, "You are a good person, like an angel of God: but the princes of the Philistines have said, He will not go down to battle with us. "Therefore get out of bed early in the morning with the other servants that are with you, and leave." David and his men rose up early in the morning to leave, and returned to the land of the Philistines. The Philistines went to Jezreel.

When David and his men got to Ziklag on the third day, the Amalekites had invaded the south, and Ziklag, and destroyed Ziklag, and burned the entire city, and had captured all the women that were there, but they didn't kill any of them, but carried them away, and then went on their way. Therefore, David and his men went to Ziklag, and it was burned with fire; and their wives, sons, and daughters were taken captive. David and his men cried until they couldn't cry anymore. David's two wives were also taken captured, Ahinoam, and Abigail. He was greatly troubled for the people talked about stoning him, because they wanted to protect their children, but David encouraged himself in the Lord his God.

David said to Abiathar the priest, Ahimelech's son, "Please, bring me the ephod." Abiathar brought the ephod to David. He sought the Lord saying, "Do You want me to find this troop, and overtake them? The Lord answered him, "Pursue: you will definitely overtake them, and without fail recover all." David and his six-hundred men went to the brook Besor, where those that were left behind stayed. He pursued, he and four-hundred men: two-hundred stayed behind, because they didn't have the strength to cross over the brook Besor.

They found an Egyptian in the field, and took him to where David was, and gave him bread, and water, and he ate it; they gave him a piece of a cake of figs, and two clusters of raisins: and when he had eaten them his strength came back to him: for he hadn't ate nor drank anything for three days and nights. David said to him, "Where are you from? Who are you?" He said, "I am a young man of Egypt, servant to an Amalekite; and my master left me, because three days ago I became very sick. We invaded the south of the Cherethites, the coast of Judah, the south of Caleb, and we burned Ziklag with fire." David said to him, "Can you take me to where your army is?" He said, "Swear to me by God, that you will not kill me, nor take me back to my master, and I will take you down to this army." When he had brought him to the army they were scattered abroad eating, drinking and dancing, because of all the things they had taken from the Philistines, and from Judah. David killed them dark unto the evening of the next day: and no one escaped except four hundred young men, which ran away on camels.

David recovered everything that the Amalekites had carried away: and he rescued his two wives, and they lacked nothing, neither small nor great, neither sons nor daughters, neither spoil, nor any thing that they had been taken from them. David recovered all. He took all the flocks and the herds, which they drove before those other cattle, and said, "This is my spoil." He went to the two hundred men, which were so weary that they could not go with him, who stayed at the brook Besor: and they went to meet David, and to meet the people that were with him: and when he came to the people he greeted them.

All the wicked men and the men of Belial of those that went with David, said, "Because they stayed behind, we will not give them anything we have, nor will we give them anything of the spoil that we have recovered, except to every man and his wife and children, that they may run them away and depart. David said, "You will not do this, my brothers, with what the Lord has given us, Who has preserved us, and delivered the company that came against us into our hand. Who will hear you concerning this? As much as the four-hundred get that went with me, so shall the two-hundred that stayed by the supplies get." Everyone get the same amount." And from that day forward, David make it a law and an ordinance for Israel until this day.

David went to Ziglag, he sent the spoil to the elders of Judah, even to his friends, saying, "Look, a present for you of the spoil of the enemies of the Lord; to them that are in Beth-el, them that are in south Ramoth, to them that are in Jattir, to them which are in Aroer, to them which are in Siphmoth, to them which are in Eshtemoa, and to them that are in Rachal, to them which are in the cities of the Jerahmeelites, to them which are in the cities of the Kenites, to them which are in Hormah, to them which are in in Chor-ashan, them which are in Athach, to them which are in Hebron, to all the places where I myself and my men were accustomed to be.

The Philistines fought against Israel: the men of Israel ran from the them, and fell dead in mount Gilboa.

The Philistines followed Saul and his sons for a long time, and they killed Jonathan, Abinadab, and Malchi-shua, which were Saul's sons.

The battle was intense against Saul and the archers found him; and they wounded him very bad.

Saul said to his armor-bearer, "Pull out your sword; and shove it thru me." so the Philistines won't torture and kill me." His armor-bearer would not do it, because he was very afraid. Therefore, he took a sword, and killed himself. When his armor-bearer saw that he was dead, he killed himself also with a sword; so Saul, his three sons, his armor-bearer, and all his men died in one day.

When the men of Israel that were on the other side of the valley, and the men that were on the other side Jordan, saw that the men of Israel ran away, and that Saul and his sons were dead, they left the cities, and the Philistines came and lived in them.

The next day when the Philistines came to strip the dead, they found Saul and his three sons dead in mount Gilboa. They cut off his head, and took off his armor and sent it to the land of the Philistines to make it know in the house of their idols, and to the people what had happened. They put his armor in Ashtaroth's house, and fastened his body against the wall of Beth-shan.

When the people of Jabesh-gilead heard what the Philistines had done to Saul, all the men of war traveled all night and took his body and his three sons bodies from the wall of Beth-shan, and went to Jabesh, and burnt them There, and took their bones, and buried them under a tree at Jabesh, and fasted seven days.

After Saul's death, when David returned from the slaughter of the Amalekites, and had stayed two days in Ziklag; this happened on the third day: a man out of Saul's camp with torn clothes and dirt on his head found David and fell to the ground and bowed down. David said to him, "Where did you come from?" He said, "Out of the camp of Israel I escaped." David said, "How did you escape? I ask of you, tell me." he answered, "The people that fought in the battle ran away, and many of them are dead; and Saul and Jonathan his son are also dead." David said, "How do you know that Saul and Jonathan are dead?" The young man said, "As I happened to be on Mount Gilboa, Saul leaned upon his spear; the chariots and horsemen followed hard after him. When he looked behind him, he saw me, and yelled at me, and I answered, "Here I am." He said, "Who are you? I answered, "I am an Amalekite." He said, "Please stand over me and kill me, for agony is come upon me, because my life is yet whole in me. I stood over him, because I was sure he could not live after he had lost the battle: and I took the crown and bracelet he was wearing and have brought them to you." David and his men grabbed the young man and tore his clothes. They mourned and wept, and fasted until evening for Saul, Jonathan, the people of the Lord, and for Israel, because they were dead. David said to the young man, "Where are you from?" He answered, "I am the son of a stranger, an Amalekite." David said, "How is it that you were not afraid to kill the Lord's anointed?" He called one of his soldiers, and said, "Go and kill this young man." The soldier did as he was told. David said unto the young man, "May your blood be upon your head; for you have said "I have killed the Lord's anointed."

David played a song for Saul and Jonathan. (He also commanded his soldiers to teach the people of Judah how to use the bow: behold, it is written in the book of Jasher (upright), (the Book of Jasher, apparently an early collection of poetic songs commemorating Israel's heroic deeds.) "The beauty of Israel has been killed upon your high places: how are the mighty fallen! Do not tell no one in Gath, do not proclaim it in the streets of Askelon, so the daughters of the Philistines will not rejoice, so the daughters of the uncircumcised do not triumph. To the mountains of Gilboa, let there be no rain nor dew fall upon you, nor fields of offerings: for it was there that the shield of the mighty is destroyed, the shield of Saul, as though he had not been anointed with oil. From the blood of the dead, from the bodies of the mighty, the bow of Jonathan did not back down, and the sword of Saul killed many. Saul and Jonathan were loved and pleasant in their lives, and at their death they were together: they were faster than eagles, they were stronger than lions.

You daughters of Israel, weep over Saul, who clothed you in scarlet, and other delightful things, who put ornaments of gold on your clothes.

How are the mighty fallen while at war! O Jonathan, you were slain in your high places. I am distressed for you, my brother Jonathan: very pleasant have you been to me: your love to me was wonderful, more than the love of women. How are the mighty fallen, and the weapons of war deceased."

After this David asked the Lord, "Do You want me to go to any of the cities of Judah?" The Lord said to him, "Yes." David asked, "What city do You want me to go?" The Lord said, "Hebron."

David went to Hebron with his two wives, Ahinoam the Jezreelitess, and Abigail Nabal's wife the Carmelite, and his men with their families: and they lived in the cities of Hebron.

The men of Judah came to him, and there they anointed David king over the house of Judah, and they told him, the men of Jabesh-gilead were the ones that buried Saul. David sent messengers to Jabesh-gilead, and said to them, "May the Lord bless you, because you have showed kindness to your lord, Saul, and have buried him; now may the Lord show kindness to you, because you have done this. Let your hands be strengthened, and be mighty: for your master Saul is dead, and the house of Judah has anointed me king over them."

Abner, the captain of Saul's host, took Ish-bosheth Saul's son over to Mahanaim; and made him king over Gilead and the Ashurites, and Jezreel, and Ephraim, and Benjamin and over all Israel.

Ish-bosheth, was forty years old when he was became king over Israel, and reigned two years. David was king over Judah. He was king in Hebron over Judah seven years and six months.

Abner, and the servants of Ish-bosheth traveled from Mahanaim to Gibeon. Joab the son of Zeruiah, and the servants of David, went to meet them by the pool of Gibeon: and they sat down, the one on the one side of the pool, and the other on the other side of the pool. Abner said to Joab, "Let the young men compete before us, and Joab said, "Let it be so." They arose and went over in groups of twelve at a time of the tribe of Benjamin, which were servants of Ish bosheth, and twelve of the servants of David. They grabbed each other by the head, and thrust their sword in each other's side; so they fell down together: that is why that place was called

Helkath-hazzurim, (interpreted The Field of Sharp Swords) which is in Gibeon. There was a very fierce battle that day; and Abner and the men of Israel were beaten.

There were three sons of Zeruiah there, Joab, Abishai, and Asahel: and Asahel could run as quick as a gazelle, and he ran after Abner; and he never stopped from pursuing him. Abner looked back, and said, "Are you Asahel?" He answered, "Yes, I am." Abner said, "Turn around and find one of the young men, and take his armor." Asahel would not do it. Asahel said again, "Do not keep following me. If you don't I will strike you to the ground. How then will I be able to hold my head up when I see your brother Joab?" He refused to turn back, so Abner with the bottom end of the spear struck him under the fifth rib, that the spear came out behind him, and he died there. Afterwards, as many as came to the place where Asahel fell dead stood still. Joab and Abishai looked for Abner: and when the day was over they were at the hill of Ammah, that was before Giah on the side of the wilderness of Gibeon. The children of Benjamin all got together and looked for Abner, and became one unit, and stood on top a hill. Abner said to Joab, "Shall the sword die forever? Do you know that there will be bitterness in the end? How long shall it be then, until you tell the people to quit pursuing their brother?" Joab said, "As God lives, if you had not spoken surely then by morning everyone would have stopped pursuing me." Therefore, Joab blew a trumpet, and all the people stood still, and pursued after Israel no more, neither did they fight anymore. Abner and his troops walked all that night through the plain, and went over Jordan, and went through all Bithron, and were at Mahanaim. Joab returned from pursuing Abner: and when he had gathered all the people together, David's servants, nineteen men and Asahel, weren't there.

The servants of David had killed three-hundred and sixty servants of Benjamin's and Abner's. They took up Asahel, and buried him in the tomb of his father, which was in Bethlehem. Joab and his men left that night, and came to Hebron at the break of day.

David and Saul were at war for a long time, and David grew stronger and stronger, but Saul grew weaker and weaker. David had children in Hebron: and his first-born was Amnon, with Ahinoam; his second, Chiliab, with Abigail; and the third, Absalom with Maacah the daughter of Talmai king of Geshur; and the fourth, Adonijah with Haggith; and the fifth, Shephatiah with Abital; and the sixth, Ithream, with Eglah his wife.

While Saul and David were fighting it was then that Abner became stronger and stronger for Saul. Saul had a prostitute, named Rizpah, the daughter of Aiah: and Ish-bosheth said to Abner, "Why did you sleep with my father's prostitute?" Abner was very angry about what Ish-bosheth had said, and he said, "Am I a dog's head, that belongs to Judah? I do show loyalty to Saul, his family, his brothers, his friends, and I have not told David where you are, and your accusing me of being with this woman? May God to this to me, and more if I do not do for David what the Lord has sworn to him; to take way the kingdom from Saul and to set up the kingdom of David over Israel and over Judah, from Dan to Beer-sheba" Ish-bosheth couldn't say anything else to Abner, because he was afraid of him.

Abner sent messengers to David on his behalf, and they told him, "Who does this land belong to? "Make a covenant with me, and I will help you all I can, to give you the land of Israel." David said, "OK, I will make a covenant with you, but one thing I require from you, and that is, you will not see me until you bring Michal, Saul's daughter to me, then you will see me."

David sent messengers to Ish-bosheth, Saul's son, and said, "Give me my wife Michal, which I bought for a hundred foreskins of the Philistines." Ish- bosheth had her taken from her husband, Phaltiel the son of Laish. Her husband followed behind her, weeping to Bahurim. Abner then said to him, "Go, return." He went back to where he was. Abner had spoken with the elders of Israel, and said, "You have been looking for David in the past to be king over you: Now then do it: because the Lord has spoken to him, saying, "By the hand of My servant David I will save My people Israel out of the hand of the Philistines, and out of the hand of all their enemies."

Abner spoke to Benjamin: and also to David in Hebron about all that seemed good to Israel, and all that seemed good to the family of Benjamin. Abner and twenty men went to David in Hebron. David made them all a feast. Abner said to David, " I will arise and go to Israel and gather all Israel to my lord the king, that they may make a covenant with you, and that you may reign over all that your heart desires. David sent him away; and he went in peace.

When the soldiers of David and Joab came back from raiding a troop, they brought a great back a great spoil; but Abner was not with David in Hebron; because he had sent him away. When Joab and all his troops came back they told Joab, "Abner, was with the king, and he has sent him away in peace." Joab went to the king and said, "What have you done? Abner came to you, why did you send him away? You know Abner came here to deceive you, and to know every move you make, and to know everything your doing." When Joab left from talking to David, he sent messengers after Abner, which brought him again from the well of Sirah: but David knew nothing about it. When Abner had came back to Hebron, Joab took him aside in the gate to speak with him privately, and stabbed him under the fifth rib, and he died, because he had killed his brother Asahel. Afterwards, when David heard of this, he said, "I and my kingdom are innocent before the Lord for ever from the blood of Abner, but let it be on Joab, and on all his father's house; and let it not fall from the family of Joab on that has a discharge, or that is a leper, or that is crippled, or that dies by the sword, or that is hungry."

Joab and Abishai his brother killed Abner, because he had killed their brother Asahel at Gibeon in a battle.

David said to Joab, and to all the people that were with him, "Rip your clothes, and put on a sackcloth, and mourn before Abner." King David followed the coffin, and they buried Abner in Hebron: and the king shouted, and wept at his grave; and all the people wept. The king mourned over him, and said, "Should Abner die as a fool dies? Your hands were not bound nor your feet put into fetters; as a man falls before wicked men, so you fell." All the people wept over him again, and when all the people came to David to persuade him to eat while it was still day, he said, "Let God do this to me, and more also if I taste bread, or anything else until the sun go down." All the people heard him say it, and it pleased them. Whatsoever the king did pleased the people. The people of Israel knew that it was not king David's intent to kill Abner. The king said to his servants, "Do you know that there was a prince and a great man killed today in Israel?

I am weak, though anointed king: and these men the sons of Zeruiah be to harsh for me: the Lord shall reward the doer of evil according to his wickedness." When Ish-bosheth heard that Abner was killed in Hebron, his hands dropped, and all the Israelites were troubled. Ish-bosheth had two men that were captains of bands: their names were Baanah, and Rechab, the sons of Rimmon a Beerothite, of the children of Benjamin: (Beeroth was considered part of the tribe of Benjamin: The Beerothites fled to Gittaim, and were sojourners there, and so it is this day.) Jonathan had a son named Mephibosheth, that was lame in his feet. He was five years old when the news of Saul and Jonathan came from Jezreel, and his nurse picked him up, and ran away: while she rushed to run away, he fell, and became lame

Rimmon the Beerothite sons, Rechab and Bannah, got to Ish-bosheth's house, in the hottest part of the day, and, he was in bed. They came into the house as though they were going to get wheat; and they stabbed him under the fifth rib and beheaded him, and took his head, and escaped through the plain. They took the head of Ish-bosheth to David in Hebron, and said to the king, "Behold the head of Ish-bosheth, your enemy, who wanted to kill you; and the Lord has avenged my lord the king today of Saul and his family." David answered Rechab and Baanah his brother, "As the Lord lives, Who has redeemed my soul out of all adversity, when someone told me, Saul is dead, thinking they had brought good news, I grabbed him, and killed him in Ziklag, who thought that I would have given him a reward for what he said. How much more, when wicked men have killed a righteous person in his own house in his bed? Shall I not therefore now require his blood of your hand, and consume you?" David commanded his servants, and they killed them, and cut off their hands and feet, and hung them up over the pool in Hebron; and they took the head of Ish-bosheth, and buried it in the tomb of Abner in Hebron.

All of the tribes of Israel went to Hebron to speak to David, and they said, "Behold, we are your bone and your flesh. In the past, when Saul was king over us, you were the one who led Israel out and brought them in; and the Lord said to you, you shall feed My people Israel, and you shall be a captain over Israel." The elders of Israel also went to Hebron to speak to the king.

King David made a covenant with them in there before the Lord: and they anointed David king over Israel.

David was thirty years old when he began his reign, and he reigned for forty years. In Hebron he reigned over Judah seven years and six months: and in Jerusalem he reigned thirty-three years over all Israel and Judah.

The king and his servants went to Jerusalem to the Jebusites, the people who lived in the land, and they told him, "Except you kill the blind and the lame, you will not come in here": thinking that he could not overpower them, but David did overpower them in Zion: and from that point on it is called the City of David. David said, "Whosoever climbs up the water shaft, and defeats the Jebusites, and the lame and the blind, that my soul hates, shall be chief and captain." They said, "The blind and the lame shall not come into the house." David lived in the fort, and called it the City of David. He built around the fort from Millo and inward. David went on, and grew great, and the Lord God of Hosts was with him. Hiram king of Tyre sent messengers to David, with cedar trees, carpenters, and masons: and they built him a house. He knew that the Lord had established him king over Israel, and that He had exalted his kingdom for His people.

David had more prostitutes and wives out of Jerusalem, after he came back from Hebron: and he had more children. These are there names of the children he had in Jerusalem: Shammuah, Shobab, Nathan, Solomon, Nepheg, Japhia, Elishama, Eliada, and Eliphalet.

When the Philistines heard that they had anointed David king over Israel, they went up to Jerusalem to find him, and when David found out they were searching for him he went out to defend himself. The Philistines also went out and spread out in the valley of Rephaim. David sought the Lord, saying, "Do you want me to fight against the Philistines? Will You deliver them into my hand?" The Lord said to David, "Go: I will without a doubt deliver the Philistines into your hand." David went to Baal-perazim, and killed them there, and he said, "The Lord has broken up my enemies before me, as the breach of waters. Therefore he called the name of that place Baal-perazim (Master of Breakthroughs). There they left their idols and David and his men burned them.

The Philistines came up yet again, and spread out in the valley of Rephaim. David sought the Lord about it, and he Lord said, "Do not go; but circle around behind them, and come upon them over against the mulberry Trees, and it shall be that when you hear the sound of marching in the tops of the mulberry trees, then you will move quickly; then will the I go out before you, to kill the army of the Philistines from Geba until you get to Gazer."

David chose thirty-thousand men of Israel, and he and the men left Baale of Judah, to get the Ark of God, Whose name is called by the name of the Lord of Hosts that sits between the cherubim. They set the Ark of God on a new cart, and brought it out of Abinadab's house that was in Gibeah: and Uzzah and Ahio, the sons of Abinadab drove the new cart, and Ahio walked in front of the Ark. David and all of Israel played music before the Lord on all kinds of instruments made of fir wood; harps, psalteries, timbrels, cornets, and on cymbals. When they came to Nachon's threshing floor, Uzzah put his hand on the Ark of God, because the oxen were shaking it. The Lord was angry at Uzzah; and God killed him there for his mistake; he died beside the Ark of God. David was angry, because of the Lord's vengeance against Uzzah: and he called the name of that place Perez-uzzah. (Outburst Against Uzzah.) David was afraid of the Lord then, and said, "How will I get the Ark of the Lord to me?" Therefore he would not bring the Ark of the Lord with him to the City of David: but he carried it to the house of Obed-edom the Gittite. The Ark of the Lord stayed at Obed-edom's house for three months, and the Lord blessed Obed-edom, and all of his family.

Someone told King David, "The Lord has blessed the house of Obed- edom, and all that he has, because the Ark of God." David went gladly and brought the Ark of God from the house of Obed-edom to the City of David, and when they had carried the Ark of the Lord six paces, he sacrificed oxen and fatlings. He danced before the Lord with all his might; and he was wearing nothing but his underwear. David and all the people of Israel brought the Ark of the Lord, shouting, and playing a trumpet; as carried the Ark of the Lord into the City of

David, Michal looked through a window, and saw the king leaping and dancing before the Lord; and she despised him in her heart. They brought in the Ark of Lord, and set it in His place, in the middle of the tabernacle that David built for it: and he offered burnt offerings and peace offerings before the Lord. When he was finished offering burnt offerings and peace offerings, he blessed the people in the name of the Lord of Hosts. He gave everyone of Israel a loaf of bread, a piece of meat, and a glass of wine; then all the people departed to their own home.

David returned home to bless his house, and Michal came out to meet him, and said, "How wonderful was the king of Israel today, who uncovered himself in front of the handmaids of his servants, as one of the base men that openly uncovers himself." He said to her, "It was before the Lord, which chose me before your dad, and before all His house, to appoint me ruler over the His people, over Israel! Therefore I will play before the Lord, and I will be a lot more undignified that this, and will be more humble in my own sight: and the maidservants that your talking about will honor me, and because of this Michal never had any children.

When the king sat in his house, and the Lord had given him rest from all his enemies, he said to Nathan the prophet, "I now live in a house made of cedar, but the Ark of God sits inside a tent behind curtains." Nathan said, "Go, do all that is in your heart to do, for the Lord is with you."

That night the Lord spoke to Nathan saying, "Go and tell My servant David, that this is what I say to him, you shall build Me a house to live in: up until now I have not lived in any house since the time that I brought the children of Israel out of Egypt; until this day I have moved about in a tabernacle in all the places that I have walked with all the children of Israel I spoke not a word with any of the tribes of Israel, whom I commanded to feed My peoplel, saying, Why don't you build Me a house of cedar? Therefore so shall you say to My servant David, this is what the Lord of Hosts says to you, I took you from the sheepfold, from following the sheep, to be a ruler over My people, over Israel: and I was with you wherever you went, and have destroyed all of your enemies out of your sight, and have made you a great name, like the name of the great men that are now dead. I will appoint a place for My people Israel, and will plant them, that they may live in a place of their own, and move no more; neither shall the children of wickedness bother them any more as they have in the past, as since the time that I commanded judges to be over My people Israel, and have given you rest from all your enemies. The Lord declares to you to build Him a house, and when you are dead, and sleep with your fathers, I will set up his seed after him, which shall be his descendants, and I will establish his kingdom. He shall build Me a house for My name, and I will establish the throne of his kingdom for ever. I will be his Father, and he shall be My son. If he commit iniquity, I will chasten him with the rod of men, and with the stripes of the children of men: but My mercy will not depart from him, as I took it from Saul, who I put away before him. Your house and your kingdom shall be established for ever before you; your throne shall be established for ever." Nathan went and told David everything he had been told and seen.

King David went in his house and sat before the Lord, and said, "Who am I, O Lord God? What is my house that You have brought me into? This was yet a small thing in Your sight, O Lord God; but You have spoken also of Your servant's house for a long time now. Is this the manner of man, O Lord God? What else can I say to You? You, Lord God, know Your servant. For Your Word's sake, and according to Your own heart, You have done all these great things, to make Your servant know them. Therefore You are great, O Lord God: for there is none like You, neither is there any God besides You, according to all that we have heard. What one nation in the world is like Your people Israel? Who You went to redeem for a people unto Yourself, and to make You a name, and to do for You great and awesome things, for Your land, before Your people which You redeemed for Yourself from the nation of Egypt, and their gods. For You have made Your people Israel Your very own for ever: and You, O Lord, have become their God. Now, O Lord God, the word that You have spoken concerning Your servant, and concerning his house, establish it for ever, and do as You have said. Let Your name be magnified forever, saying, The Lord of Hosts is the God over Israel: and let the house of Your servant David be established before You; for You, O Lord of Hosts, God of Israel, have revealed to Your servant, saying, I will build you a house: therefore has Your servant found it in his heart to pray this prayer to You; now,

O Lord God, You are that God, and Thy words be true, You have promised this goodness to Your servant: because of this let it please You to bless the house of Your servant, that it may continue for ever before You: for You, O Lord God, have spoken it: and with Your blessing let the house of Your servant be blessed for ever.

Afterwards, David defeated the Philistines, and humiliated them: he took the land of Metheg-ammah away from the Philistines, and also defeated Moab. Forcing them down to the ground, he measured them off with a rope; with two lines he measured off those to be put to death, and with one full line those to be kept alive. The Moabites became David's servants, and brought gifts to him. He also defeated Hadadezer, the son of Rehob, king of Zobab, as he went to widen his territory to the river Euphrates. David took from him 1,000 chariots, 7,000 horsemen, and 20,000 footmen; and he cut the back hamstrings of the rear legs from all the chariot horses, but did not cut 100 chariots hamstrings. When the Syrians of Damascus came to help Hadadezer, David killed 220,000 Syrians. Then he put garrisons in Syria of Damascus: and the they became servants of his, and brought gifts to him. The Lord preserved David, and gave him victory wherever he went. David took the shields of gold that were on the servants of Hadadezer, and brought them to Jerusalem; from Betah, and from Berothai, cities of Hadadezer, he took an extreme amount of brass. Toi king of Hamath heard that David had killed all the armies of Hadadezer, he sent Joram his son to king David, to ask him how he was doing, and to bless him, because he had fought against Hadadezer, and defeated him: for Hadadezer had battles with Toi. Joram, brought back with him articles of silver, articles of gold, and articles of brass: David dedicated these to the Lord, along with silver and gold that he had dedicated from all nations which he conquered. Of Syria, Moab, Ammonites, the Philistines, Amalek, and from the spoil of Hadadezer. David made himself a name when he returned from killing the Syrians in the valley of salt, having 18,000 men.

He put garrisons in all Edom, and everyone in Edom became David's servants. The Lord preserved him wherever he went, and reigned over all Israel; and he executed judgment and justice to all the his people. Joab was over the army; and Jehoshaphat was the recorder. Zadok, and Ahimelech, were the priests; Shavsha was the secretary; and Benaiah was over both the Cherethites and the Pelethites; and David's sons were priests.

David said, "Is there anything else that is left from the house of Saul, that I may show him that I am faithful to our covenant for Jonathan's sake?" There was a servant whose name was Ziba from Saul's house, and when they had brought him to David, the he said to him, "Are you Ziba?" He said, "Your servant is he." The king said, "Is there anyone from Saul's house that I may show the kindness of God to him?" Ziba said, "Jonathan has a son, which is lame." The king said to him, "Where is he?" Ziba said, "He is in Machir's house, the son of Ammiel, in Lo-debar. King David had his servants bring Merib-baal to him. When he was with David, he bowed down in front of him. David said to him, "Merib-baal." He answered, "Behold, your servant!" David said, "Do not be afraid, because I will show you kindness for Jonathan your father's sake, and will restore to you all the land of Saul your grandfather; and you shall eat bread at my table continually."

The king called for Ziba, and said, "I have given to your master's son all that belongs to Saul and to all his house. You therefore, and your sons, and your servants, shall work in the land for him, and you shall bring in the fruits so that your master's son may have food to eat, but Merib-baal shall eat bread always at my table." Ziba had fifteen sons and twenty servants. Ziba said to the king, "According to all that my lord and king has commanded his servant, so shall your servant do." "As for Merib-baal," said the king, "he shall eat at my table, as one of the king's sons." Merib-baal had a young son, whose name was Micha, and all of Ziba's family were servants to Merib-baal. Merib-baal lived in Jerusalem: for he did eat every meal at the king's table, and was lame in both of his feet.

Afterwards, the king of the Ammonites died, and Hanun, his son reigned in his place. David said, "I will be king to Hanun the son of Nahash, the same way his father was king to me, and he sent his servants to comfort Hanun, because of his father. David's servants went to the land of the children of Ammon. The princes of the children of Ammon said to Hanun their lord, "Do you think that David is honoring your father by sending people to comfort you? We think he is sending his servants here to search the city, and to spy it out and to defeat us." Therefore Hanun took David's servants and shaved off half of their beards, and cut their clothes in half, all the way to their buttocks, and sent them away.

When David found out about this, he had someone meet them, because they were very ashamed, he said, "Wait in Jericho until your beards grow back, and them come home."

The children of Ammon saw that what they did made David very angry, and they hired the Syrians of Beth-rehob, the Syrians of Zoba, 20,000 soldiers of king Maachah 1,000 men, and of Ish-tob 12,000 men. When David knew this, he sent Joab, and all of his mighty men.

The children of Ammon came out and prepared for battle in front of the gate. The Syrians of Zoba, Rehob, Ish-tob, and Maacah were by themselves in the field.

Joab saw that there were lines of soldiers in front of him and behind him, he chose the best soldiers of Israel, and prepared them to fight against the Syrians. The rest of the people he put his brother Abishai be in charge of, so he could prepare them to fight the children of Ammon. He said, "If the Syrians be to powerful for my men, then you will come and help me, but if the children of Ammon be too powerful for your men, then I will come and help you, be of good courage, and let us be strong men for our people, and for the cities of our God: and may the Lord do what is good from Him." When Joab and his army were close to the Syrians in battle the they ran away from him. The children of Ammon saw the Syrians run away, they also ran away from Abishai, and went to the city. Joab returned from fighting with the children of Ammon and went to Jerusalem. The Syrians know that they had been defeated by Israel, and they all gathered together.

Then Hadarezer sent men and brought out the Syrians that were beyond the river: and they went to Helam; and Shobach, the captain of the army of Hadarezer went before them.

When David found out about this he brought all of Israel together, and went over Jordan, to Helam. The Syrians prepared for battle against David and fought against him. They fled away from Israel; David killed 700 charioteers of the Syrians, and 40,000 horsemen, and he also killed Shobach the captain of their army. When all the kings saw that they were servants to Hadarezer saw that they were defeated by Israel, they made peace with Israel, and served them. The Syrians were afraid to help the children of Ammon any more.

In the spring of the year, at the time when kings go to battle, David sent Joab, his servants, and all of Israel, and they destroyed the children of Ammon, and besieged Rabbah. David waited in Jerusalem. One evening he got out of bed, and walked on the roof of his house: and from the roof he saw a woman taking a bath, and she was a very beautiful woman. David sent a messenger to find out more about this woman. Someone said, "Isn't this Bath-sheba, Eliam's daughter, Uriah the Hittite's wife?" David then sent messengers to bring her to him, and she went. They slept together, she was cleansed from her monthly cycle, and she returned to her home. She had a child, and sent someone to tell David saying, "I am pregnant." David sent word to Joab saying, "Send me Uriah the Hittite," and Joab sent him to David. When Uriah was at David's house, he asked Uriah how Joab and his men were doing, and how the war was going. David said to Uriah, "Go down to your house, and wash your feet." Uriah left the king's house with a gift of food, but he slept at the door of the king's house with all the king's servants, but did not go to his own house. When they had told David that Uriah did not go home, he said to Uriah, "Didn't you come from a journey? Why didn't you go to your home?" Uriah said, "The Ark, along with Israel and Judah are sleeping in tents; and my lord Joab, the servants of my lord, are camped out in open fields; shall I then go into my home, to eat and drink, and to sleep with my wife? As long as you live, and your soul lives I will not do this." David said, "Wait here today, and tomorrow I will let you leave." Therefore Uriah stayed in Jerusalem that day and the next day. When David had called for him; he ate and drank before David, and he made him drunk: that evening he went out to lay on his bed with the servants of his lord, but did not go to his home. The next morning, David wrote a letter to Joab, and gave it to Uriah to give to him. He wrote in the letter, "Put Uriah in the forefront of the fiercest battle, and leave him alone there, that he may be killed." Afterwards, while Joab was guarding the city, he assigned Uriah a place where he knew that strong men of war were at. The men of the city went out and fought with Joab: and some of the people of the servants of David died, and Uriah died also. Joab sent a messenger to David to tell him everything about the war; and told him "When you have told the king everything about the war if he is angry, and he says to you, "How close were you to the city when you began to fight? Didn't you know that they would shoot from the wall? Who killed Abimelech? Didn't a woman throw a piece of a millstone on him from the wall, and he died in Thebez? Why did you go near the wall?" Then say to him, "Your servant Uriah is also dead." The messenger went, and told David all that Joab had said to him. The messenger said to David, "Truly the men fought against us, and came out against us in the field, and we were with them in front of the gate. The shooters shot from off the wall at your servants; and some of your men; and some of the king's men are dead, and your servant Uriah the Hittite is also dead." David said to the messenger, "This is what I want you to say to Joab, Don't let this bother you, for the sword devours one as well as another: make your battle stronger against the city, and overtake it: and you encourage him." When the wife of Uriah heard that he was dead, she mourned for him. When her mourning had ended, David sent for her to come to his house, and she became his wife, and bare him a son. What David had done, displeased the Lord.

The Lord sent Nathan to David. When Nathan and David were together, Nathan said to him, "There were two men in one city, one was rich and the other poor. The rich man had an extreme amount of flocks and herds: but the poor man had nothing except one little ewe lamb, which he had bought and raised: and it grew up together with him, and with his children, and it ate his food and drank his water and he took care of it, and it was like a daughter to him. There came a traveler to the rich man, and he refused to give him any sheep from his flock to prepare for the wayfaring man that came to him; but instead he took the poor man's lamb and prepared it for the man that had come to him." David was very angry with the man; and he said to Nathan, "As the Lord lives, the man that has done this deserves to die. He shall restore the lamb fourfold, because he has done this, and because he had no pity." Nathan said to David, "You are the man. This is what the Lord God of Israel wants you to know, I anointed you king over Israel, and I took you out of Saul's hand; and I gave you your master's house, and your master's wives to be your own, and gave you the house of Israel and of Judah; and if that had been too little, I would moreover have given you much more; so why have you despised the commandment of the Lord, to do evil in His sight? You have killed Uriah with a sword, and have taken his wife to be your wife, and you have let the children of Ammon kill him; because you have done this, the sword shall never leave your house, because you have despised Me, and have taken the wife of Uriah to be your wife. This is what the Lord says, Behold, I will let adversity raise up against you out of your own house, and I will take your wives from you, and give them to your neighbor, and he shall lie with them in the daylight; for you did it secretly: but I will do this thing before all Israel, and in broad daylight."

David said, "I have sinned against the Lord." Nathan said, "The Lord has also put away your sin; you will not die, but because you have done this, you have given great occasion to the enemies of the Lord to blaspheme. The child that was born will die."

Nathan left and returned to his house. The Lord allowed a disease to come on the child that Uriah's wife had with David, and it was very sick. David then pleaded with God for the child; and he fasted, and went in, and laid on the ground all night. Then the elders that lived with him got out of bed, to get him up off the ground, but he would not get up, neither would he eat bread with them. Seven days later the child died. His servants was afraid to tell him that the child was dead: for they said, "While the child was alive, we talked with him, and he would not listen to us: how will he harm himself if we tell him that the child is dead?" When David saw that his servants were whispering, he perceived that the child was dead: therefore he said to his servants, "Is the child dead?" They said, "He is dead." David got up from the ground, and took a bath, and anointed himself, changed his clothes, and came into the house of the Lord, and worshiped: afterwards he went to his own house; and when he wanted something to eat, they gave him food. His servants said to him, "What have you done? You fasted and wept for the child, while it was alive; but when the child died, you got up off the ground and ate." He said, "While the child was alive, I fasted and wept: for I said, Who can tell whether the Lord will be gracious to me, that the child may live?; now that he is dead, why should I fast? Can I bring him back again? I will go to him, but he will not come back to me."

David comforted Bath-sheba his wife, and slept with her, and she bore him a son, and he named him Solomon, and the Lord loved him. David sent a message to Nathan the prophet about his son, and Nathan called the child, Jedidiah, (which means Beloved of the Lord) because of the Lord.

Joab fought against Rabbah of the children of Ammon, and took the royal city. He sent messengers to David saying, "I have fought against Rabba, and have taken the city of water; now gather everyone together and encamp the city, and take it: because if you don't I will take the city, and it shall be mine." David gathered all the people together, and went to Rabbah, and fought against it, and took it. He took their king's crown off of his head, and the weight of the crown was one talent of gold ($ 5,760,000) with the precious stones; and it was set on David's head. He brought with him an abundant supply of goods from the city, and took the people of that city and put them under saws, under iron harrows, and under iron axes, and made them cross over the brick work: he also did this to everyone in the other cities of the children of Ammon. Afterwards, David and the children of Israel returned to Jerusalem.

Absalom, David's son had a beautiful sister named Tamar; and Amnon, David's son loved her. Amnon was so distressed, that he was sick because of his sister Tamar; for she was a virgin; he didn't think it was right for him to do anything to her, but he had a friend named Jonadab, Shimeah son, David's brother. Jonadab was a very crafty man. Jonadab said to Amnon, "Why are you, the king's son, getting skinner every day? Are you going to tell me or not?" Amnon said, "I love Tamar, my brother Absalom's sister." Jonadab said to him, "Go lay down on your bed, and act like your sick: and when your father comes to see you, tell him, please let my sister Tamar come, and bake me a couple of cakes, and prepare them in front of me, and let me eat it out of her hand."

So Amnon lay down, and pretended to be sick: and when the king came to see him, Amnon said to the king, "I ask of you, let Tamar my sister come, and make me a couple of cakes in my sight, that I may eat them out of her hand." David sent word to Tamar saying, "Go to your brother Amnon's house and make him something to eat." When Tamar got to Amnon's house, he was laying down. She took flour, and kneaded it, and made cakes in front of him, and baked them. She poured them out into a pan in front of him; but he refused to eat. He said, "Everyone leave;" and everyone went away. Then he said to Tamar, "Bring me the food into the bedroom, so I can eat it out of your hand." Tamar took the cakes that she had made into Amnon's bedroom. When she brought them to him, he grabbed her, and said to her, "Come and lay down with me, my sister." She said, "No, my brother, do not force me; for no such thing ought to be done in Israel: don't do this disgraceful thing. Where could I take this shame? As for you, you shall be like one of the stupid fools in Israel. I beg of you talk to the king; for he will not withhold me from you." Amnon would not listen to her, but being stronger than her, he raped her. Amnon hated her with a very great hatred. The hatred that he felt toward her was greater than the love that he had felt for her. He said, "Get up, and leave." She said, "There is no cause for sending me away. You want me to leave more than you wanted to make love to me." He would not listen to her. He called his servant that helped him, and said, "Get this woman away from me, and bolt the door after she is gone." she was wearing a robe of many colors: for with such robes the king's daughters wore that were virgins. His servant took her out of the house, and bolted the door behind her. Tamar put ashes on her head, tore her robe, and put her hand on her head and started crying.

Absalom her brother asked her, "Has Amnon your brother been with you? Don't answer me yet, my sister: he is your brother; don't take what he has done to heart." Therefore Tamar kept silent while she was in Absalom's house. When king David heard about what had happened, he was very angry.

Absalom went and talked with his brother Amnon neither good nor bad: for he hated his brother, because he had raped his sister Tamar.

After two years had passed, Absalom had sheepshearers in Baal-hazor, which is beside Ephraim: and he asked all the king's sons to come with him to Baal-hazor. He went to the king and said, "Look, your servant has sheepshearers; I ask of you please come and all your servants to, with me." The king said, "No, my son I don't want all of us to be a burden to you." He asked him again, but he would not go, but blessed him. Then Absalom said, "If you won't go, I ask of you to let my brother Amnon go with us." The king said, him, "Why should he go with you?" Absalom kept asking him to let Amnon and all of the king's sons go with him.

Absalom told his servants, "Pay attention to Amnon, when he gets drunk from the wine, I will say to you kill him; then kill him, don't be afraid: because I have commanded you. Be courageous, and be like sons of valor." Absalom's servants did to Amnon as he had commanded them. All of the king's sons stood up, and every man got on his mule and ran away. While they were on their way back home, someone told David that Absalom had killed all of the king's sons, and there is not one of them is alive. The king stood up, tore his clothes, and lay on the ground; and all of his servants stood by with their clothes tore. Jonadab, the son of Shimeah, David's brother, said, "My lord don't think that they have killed all of the you sons; for Amnon is the only one that is dead: this has happened because Absalom commanded us, because Amnon raped his sister. My lord don't think that all of the your sons are dead: Amnon is the only one dead."

Absalom ran away, and the young man that kept watch raised his head and saw many people coming up over the hillside behind him. Jonadab said to the king, "Look, your sons are coming: just like your servant said." After he had finished saying that, the king's sons came, yelling and weeping; and the king and all his servants wept bitterly, but Absalom ran away, and went to Talmai, the son of Ammihud's, king of Geshur. He lived there for three years. David mourned for his son every day. King David wanted very much to go to Absalom: because he was comforted concerning Amnon, seeing he was dead.

Joab knew that the king was concerned about Absalom, so he sent a messenger to Tekoah, to bring back to him a wise woman, and he said to her, "I ask of you, pretend to be a mourner, and put on mourning clothes, and do not anoint yourself with oil, but act like a woman that has mourned because of someone's death for a long time, and go to the king and tell him this." Joab told her exactly what to say.

When the woman of Tekoah spoke to the king, she fell on her face, and showed him respect, and said, "Help, O king." The king said to her, "What troubles you?" She answered, "I am indeed a widow woman, and my husband is dead. Your handmaid has two sons, and they fought against each other in the field, and there was no one to separate them, but one them struck the other, and killed him, and the whole family is risen up against your handmaid, and they said, Give us your son that killed his brother, that we may kill him, and we will kill the heir also: so they shall extinguish my anger that I am feeling, and then the world will not even know my husband was alive." The king said to the woman, "Go to your home now, and I will give the command on what shall happen to you." The woman said, "My lord, O king, may the guilt be on me and my father's house, and may you and your throne be guiltless." The king said, "Whoever says anything to you, bring him to me, and he will not say anything to you anymore." She said, "I ask of you, remember the Lord thy God, and do not allow the avenger of blood to kill any more, so they won't kill my son." He said, "As the Lord lives, there will not be one hair from your son's head fall to the ground." The woman said, "I ask of you let your handmaid speak one word to my lord the king." He said, "Say on." The woman said, "Why then have you thought such a thing against the people of God? You talk like he is guilty of this thing, in that you do bring home his banished. We must all die, and are as water spit on the ground, which cannot be gathered up again; neither does God take anyone's life: yet He makes a way that His banished children are not taken away from Him. Therefore that is why I am come here to talk to you. It's because the people have made me afraid: and I said, I will now speak to the king; the king may do what I ask of him. I know the king will listen to me, and deliver me out of the hands of the man that would take me and my son both out of the inheritance of God. Then I said, the word of my lord, the king will be comforting: my lord the king is like an angel of God, he knows what is good and bad: therefore the Lord thy God will be with you." The king answered the woman, "Please do not hide anything from me that I ask you." The woman said, "Let my lord the king now speak." The king said, "Didn't Joab put you up to this?" The woman answered and said, "As your soul lives, my lord the king, no one can turn to the right hand or to the left from anything that my lord the king has spoken: for your servant Joab, he asked me to do this, and he told me what to say: and my lord is wise, like an angel of God, and knows all things that are in the earth." The king said to Joab, "All right now, I will allow this to happen: go and bring the young man Absalom home." Joab fell to the ground on his face, and blessed the king: and he said, "Today your servant knows that he has found grace in your sight, my lord, O king, because you have done what your servant has asked of you." Joab got up and went to Geshur, and brought Absalom to Jerusalem. The king said, "Let him return to his own house, and don't allow him to see me." Absalom returned to his home, and did not see the king.

There was not a more handsome man in Israel than Absalom, and everyone told him. There was no flaw on his body, and when he cut his hair, (he would cut it at the end of every year because it became to heavy) he would weigh it, and it weighed 200 shekels (5 pounds). He always used the standard weights that were used in the palace.

Absalom had three sons, and one daughter, whose name was Tamar: she was a beautiful woman. He lived in Jerusalem for two years, but never saw the king. He sent someone to Joab, to tell him he wanted to see the king, but Joab wouldn't come to see him: and when he sent someone the second time, he still would not come and see him. He said to his servants, "Notice that Joab's field is near to mine, and he has barley there; go and set it on fire. Absalom's servants set it on fire."

Joab went to Absalom's house and said to him, "Why did you tell your servants to set my field on fire?" Absalom answered, "I sent word to you, saying, Come to me, I want you to go to the king and tell him, why did you want me to move from Geshur? It would be good for me to still be there. I want to see you and if I have done anything wrong at all, then kill me." Therefore Joab went to the king and told him what Absalom had told him to say, and when the king wanted to see Absalom, Absalom then went to him, and bowed down on his face in front of the king: and the king kissed him.

Afterwards, Absalom got chariots and horses ready, and fifty men to run before him. He got out of bed early in the morning and stood beside the entrance of the gate of the city: so that when any man that brought a lawsuit to the king for judgment, He would ask him, "What city are you from?" The man would answer him, "Your servant is from one of the tribes of Israel."

Absalom would say unto him, "Your claim is good and right; but the king has no deputy to hear your case. "I wish that I were made a judge in the land, so that every man that had any lawsuit or cause would come to me, and I would give him justice." So it was, that when any man came near him and bowed down to him, he would stretch out his hand, and take him and kiss him. He would do this to every man that came to the king for judgment: he stole the hearts of the men of Israel.

After four years, Absalom said to the king, "I ask of you, let me go and pay my vow, that I have vowed to the Lord, in Hebron. because I vowed a vow while I lived in Geshur in Syria; saying, If the Lord will bring me back to Jerusalem, then I will serve the Him." The king said to him, "Go in peace." Absalom left and went to Hebron.

Absalom sent spies throughout all the tribes of Israel, saying, "As soon as you hear the sound of a trumpet, then I want you to say, Absalom reigns in Hebron." Absalom and 200 men that he invited, went out of Jerusalem, and they went innocent, because they knew nothing. Absalom sent someone to get Ahithophel the Gilonite, David's counselor, from Giloh, while he offered sacrifices. The conspiracy was strong; the people grew in number with Absalom.

A messenger went to David and told him, "The men of Israel are following Absalom." David said to all of his servants that were with him in Jerusalem, "Get up, and let us go; because we will not escape from Absalom: hurry up and leave, so he won't suddenly overpower us, and bring us disaster, and kill every person in the city with a sword." The king's servants said, "Now, your servants are ready to do whatever you shall command." The king and all of his household left. He left ten women, which were prostitutes, to take care of the house. He and all of the people with him waited in a place far away. All of his servants out ran him; and the Cherethites, and the Pelethites, and the Gittites, all 600 men that went with him from Gath, out ran the him. Then he said to Ittai the Gittite, "Why are you going with us?" Go home, and stay with the king (Absalom): because you are a foreigner, and also an exile from your own place. In fact you came only yesterday, should I today make you wander around with us?; seeing I go where want to go; return to your own place, and take back your brothers: may mercy and truth be with you." Ittai answered the king, "As the Lord lives, and as my lord the king lives, I will for sure be where my lord the king is, either dead or alive." David answered him, "Go and cross over." Ittai passed over, all his men, and all the little ones that were with him. Everyone in the country cried loudly, and all the people and the king also crossed over the brook Kidron, toward the wilderness. Zadok, and all the Levites were with him, packing the Ark of the Covenant of God: they sat the Ark of God down, and Abiathar went up on a mountain until all the people had gotten out of the city.

The king said to Zadok, "Carry the Ark of God back into the city: if I find grace with the Lord, He will bring me back to the city, and will show me both it and His habitation: but if He says, 'I have no delight in you', here I am, let Him do to me what He sees fit. Aren't you a prophet? Go back to the city in peace, and with your two sons, Ahimaaz your son, and Jonathan Abiathar's son. I will wait in the plain of the wilderness until someone tells me what you want me to do." Therefore Zadok and Abiathar carried the Ark of God back to Jerusalem: and they waited there.

And David went up by the Ascent of Mount Olivet, and crying with his head covered, and he went barefooted. All the people that were with him covered their head, and followed him also crying. Someone told him, "Ahithophel is one of the conspirators with Absalom." David said, "O Lord, I ask of you, turn the plans of Ahithophel into foolishness.

When David had come to the top of the Mount, where he worshiped God, Hushai the Archite came to meet him with his coat tore, and dirt on his head. David told him, "If you go on with me, then you will be a burden to me; but if you return to the city, and say to Absalom, I will be your servant, O king, as I have been your dad's servant up until now, so I will now be your servant also: then may you defeat the plans of Ahithophel for me. Zadok and Abiathar the priests will be there with you; and whatever you hear from the king's house, that is what I want you to tell Zadok and Abiathar; and there with them are their two sons, Ahimaaz, and Jonathan. Tell them to come and tell me every thing that you hear." Hushai, David's friend went back to the city, and Absalom went to Jerusalem.

When David had gotten a little past the top of the hill he met Ziba the servant of Mephibosheth, with a couple of donkeys saddled, carrying 200 loaves of bread, 100 bunches of raisins, 100 summer fruits and a container of wine. He said to Ziba, "What are you going to do with all of this?" Ziba said, "The donkeys are for the king's household to ride on; the bread and summer fruit are for the young men to eat; and the wine is for anyone that is faint in the wilderness." The king said, "Where is your master's son?" Ziba said, "He is in Jerusalem, because he said, Today Israel shall give me the kingdom that my father once had.'" The king said, "Here, all that Mephibosheth has belongs to you." Ziba said, "I humbly ask of you that I find favor with you, my lord, O king."

When king David arrived in Bahurim, there was a man of the family of Saul that came out to meet him, whose name was Shimel, the son of Gera: he cursing as he came out to meet him, and throwing stones at David, and his servants with all the people and all the mighty men were on his right and left side. He said when he cursed, "Come out, come out you bloodthirsty man, you reprobate. The Lord has brought all of the blood of the family of Saul upon you, in whose place you reigned; and the Lord has given the kingdom to Absalom you son: and now your mischief has caught up with you, because you are a bloodthirsty man." Then Abishai the son of Zeruiah asked the king, "Why should this dead dog curse my lord the king? Let me go over there and cut his head off." The king said, "What have I to do with you, you sons of Zeruiah? Let him curse, because the Lord has said to him, Curse David. Who will say, Why have you done this?'" David said to Abishai, and his servants, "See how my own son, which came from my own body, wants to kill me? How much more now is this Benjamite wanting do it? Leave him alone, and let him curse; for the Lord has allowed him. It may be that the Lord will look on my affliction, and that He will repay me with good things for this man's cursing today." David and his men walked down the road, and Shimel went along the hillside following him, and cursed him, and threw rocks at him, and kicked dust on him. The king and all the people that were with him were tired, and rested there.

Absalom, and all the people, the men of Israel, went to Jerusalem, and Ahithophel was also with him. When Hushai, David's friend meet Absalom, He said to him, "Long live the king, long live the king." Absalom said to Hushai, "Is this how you show loyalty to your friend? Why didn't you go with your friend?" Hushai said, "No: but who the Lord, and these people, and all the men of Israel, choose, his will I be, and I will stand by him. Who should I serve? Should it not be his son, as I have served your father, so shall I serve you." Absalom said to Ahithophel, "Give us some advice as to what we should do." Ahithophel said to him, "Go into your father's home and have sex with his prostitutes, that he has left there to take care of the palace, and everybody in Israel will hear that you are hated of your father: then the hands of all your supporters will be strong." They set up a tent for Absalom on top of the palace; and he went and had sex with his father's prostitutes, and all of Israel knew it. The advice of Ahithophel, which he advised in those days, was as if a man had gotten clear direction from God: so was all the advice that Ahithophel gave both to David and Absalom.

Ahithophel said to Absalom, "Let me pick out 12,000 men, and I will go and look for David tonight; and I will find him when he is weary and weak Handed. I will make him tremble with fear: and all the people that are with him shall run away; and I will attack only the king: and I will bring all of the people to you: when everyone returns except the man whom you seek: so all the people shall be in peace." What Ahithophel said please Absalom greatly, and all of the elders of Israel. Absalom said, "Call for Hushai also, and let us hear what he has to say to." Hushai came to Absalom, he said to him, "This is what Ahithophel has said, should we do what he says? If not then tell me." Hushai said, "The advice that Ahithophel has given is not good at this time. For you know your father and his men are mighty men, and they are enraged in their minds, as a bear that has been robbed of her cubs in the field: and your father is a man of war, and he will not camp with the people. Surely by now he is hid in some pit, or in some other place: and it shall be when some of them are overpowered by the first, that whoever hears about it will say, the people that follow Absalom are being killed. Them that are valiant whose heart is like that of a lion, shall melt: because everyone in Israel knows that your father is a mighty man, and the men that are with him are valiant. The advice that I give to you is that everyone in Israel be brought to you, from Dan to Beer-sheba, as the sand that is by the sea, a multitude; and that you go to battle in person. We will find him wherever he is, and we will fall on him, as the dew falls on the ground: him and all the men that are with him shall die. Moreover, if he is in a city, then all of Israel will bring ropes to that city, and we will pull it into the river, until there be not one small stone found there." Absalom and all the men of Israel said, "The advice of Hushai is better than the advice of Ahithophel. the Lord has purposely defeated the good advice of Ahithophel, so that He could bring evil to Absalom.

Hushai said to Zadok and Abiathar the priests, "This is what Ahithophel advised Absalom and the elders of Israel to do: and this is what I told them. Therefore send someone now to tell David, Do not spend the night in the plains of the wilderness, but hurry and cross over, so the king and the men that are with him will not die.'"

Jonathan and Ahimaaz stayed in En-rogel, because they didn't want to be seen coming into the city. A maidservant went and told them; and they went and told king David. A little boy saw them and told Absalom: but they ran away quickly, and went to a man's house in Bahurim, which had a well in his yard; where they went down. The woman took a spread and covered the mouth of the well, and spread grain on it, and no one knew what had happened. When Absalom's servants came to the house, they said to the woman, "Where is Ahimaaz and Jonathan?" She said, "They are gone over the brook of water." When they had looked for them and could not find them, they returned to Jerusalem. After the servants had left, they came up out of the well, and went and told king David, "Get up, and cross over the water quickly: for such and such is Ahithophel advice against you." David and all of his men got up and crossed over Jordan. By morning light everyone that was with him had crossed over.

Ehen Ahithophel saw that his advice was not followed, he saddled his donkey, and went to his house, to the city where he was from, and put his house in order, and hung himself, and was buried in the tomb of his father.

David went to Mahanaim, and Absalom and all the men of Israel crossed over Jordan. Absalom made Amasa captain instead of Joab: Amasa was the son of Jether and Israelite, who had been Abigail's lover, the daughter of Nahash, sister to Zeruiah Joab's mother.

Absalom and the men of Israel camped in the land of Gilead. When David had arrived in Mahanaim, that Shobi the son of Nahash of Rabbah of the children of Ammon, and Machir the son of Ammiel of Lo-debar, and Barzillai the Gileadite of Rogelim brought beds and basins, pots, wheat, barley, flour, parched grain, beans, lentils, parched seeds, honey, butter, sheep, and cheese, for him, and the people that were with him to eat: because someone had said, "These people are hungry, tired and thirsty in the wilderness."

David had all the people that were with him numbered, and appointed captains over thousands, and captains over a hundred. He sent out one-third of his men under the guidance of Joab, and another one-third under the guidance of Abishai, and one third under the guidance of Ittai. The king said to all of the people, "I myself shall also go with you;" but the people answered, "You shall not go with us: for if we run away, they will not care about us; neither if half of us die: but you are worth 10,000 of us: therefore it is better that you help us out of the city." The king said, "Whatever seems best to you is what I'll do." He stood by the gate side, and all the people came out by hundreds and by thousands. The king commanded Joab, Abishai and Ittai, saying, "Be gentle for my sake with the young man, Absalom." All the people heard when the king told the captains what they should do concerning Absalom. The people went out into the field to fight with Israel: and the battle was in the forest in Ephraim; where the people of Israel were killed before the servants of David, and there were 20,000 men died that day. The battle was scattered all over the face of all the country: and the forest killed more people that day than the sword.

Absalom met the servants of David, and he rode on a mule, and the mule went under the thick branches of a great oak, and his head caught hold of the oak, and he was stuck in the tree, he was left hanging: and the mule that he was riding went away. A certain man saw it and went and told Joab, "I saw Absalom hanging in a tree." Joab said, "You just saw him! Why didn't you knock him to the ground? I would have given you ten shekels of silver, ($ 1,280) and a belt." The man said, "Though I should receive 1,000 shekels of silver ($ 128,000) in my hand, yet I would not raise my hand to harm the king's son. We heard what the king said to you, Abishai, and Ittai when he told you three, do not harm the young man Absalom. On the other hand, I should have pretended like I was dead: for there is nothing kept secret from the king, and you yourself wouldn't have had anything to do with me." Joab said, "I will not wait around here with you." He took three spears in his hand, and drove them through Absalom's heart, while he was still alive, hanging in the oak tree. When the ten young men that packed Joab's armor surrounded Absalom, and killed him. Joab blew the trumpet, and the people returned from running after Israel, because Joab held them back. They took Absalom, and threw him into a great big pit in the forest, and piled rocks on him, and all Israel ran to their tents. Absalom before his death had put up a pillar in the king's valley: for he said, "I have no son to carry on my name: and he called the pillar after his own name: and it is called Absalom's monument to this day.

Ahimaaz said, "Let me run now, and give the king the news, how that the Lord has delivered him from his enemies." Joab said, "You shall not tell him anything today, but you can tell him some other day: today you will tell him nothing, because the king's son is dead." Joab said to Cushi, "Go and tell the king what you have seen." Cushi bowed before Joab, and ran. Ahimaaz said to Joab again, "Be what it may, I ask of you, let me also run after Cushi." Joab said, "Why would you run, my son, seeing that you don't have any news to tell?" Ahimaaz said, "Whatever may come of it, let me run, and Joab said to him, "Run." Ahimaaz ran through the plain, and outran Cushi.

David sat between the two gates: and the watchman went up to the roof over the gate to the wall, looked up, and saw a man running by himself. The watchman cried, and told the king. The king said, "If he is alone, he has some news." He ran quickly, and was getting closer. The watchman saw another man running: and the watchman yelled at the gatekeeper, "Look another man is running by himself." The king said, "He also brings good news." The watchman said, "I think the first man is Ahimaaz." The king said, "He is a good man, and comes with good news."

Ahimaaz crying out to the king said, "All is well," and he fell down on the ground face first before the king, and said, "Blessed be the Lord thy God, which has delivered the men that took up arms against my lord the king." The king said, "Is the young man Absalom safe?" Ahimaaz answered, "When Joab sent your servant, and me thy servant, I saw a great tumult, but I didn't know what it was." The king said, "Turn to your side, and stand there." So he did.

Cushi came up and said, "Tidings, my lord the king: for the Lord has delivered you today of all them that rose up against you." The king said, "Is the young man Absalom safe? Cushi answered, "The enemies of my lord the king, and all that rise against him to do him harm, be as that young man is." The king was very moved, and went up to the chamber over the gate, and cried: and as he was leaving he said, "O my son Absalom, my son, my son Absalom! I wish God would have allowed me to die instead of you, O Absalom, my son, my son."

Joab was told, "The king is crying and mourning for Absalom." The victory that day was turned into mourning for everyone: for the people heard that day that the king was grieving over his son. They made their way back that day to the city, as people being ashamed do when they run away from battle. The king covered his face, and cried with a loud voice saying, 'O my son Absalom, O Absalom, my son, my son!'" Joab went to the king's house, and said, "Today you have disgraced all of your servants, that have saved your life, and the lives of your sons, daughters, wives, and concubines, because you have loved your enemies and hated your friends. You have made it known today, that you have no respect for princes nor servants. I think that if Absalom had lived, and all of us had died today, then you would have been pleased. Go, and speak to the heart of your servants: for I swear to God, if you don't go and speak to them, everyone will leave you tonight: and that will be the worst thing that has ever happened to you. The king got up, and sat at the town door. All of his followers were told, "Look, the king is sitting at the town door." All the people came before the king: for Israel had ran to their tents.

All the tribes of Israel were in a dispute with one another, saying, "The king saved us from our enemies, and he delivered us from the Philistines; and now he has ran out of the land for Absalom, whom we anointed over us, that died in battle; because of this, why is no one talking about bringing the king back?" King David sent the priests to Zadok and Abiathar saying, "Talk to the elders of Judah, and tell them, 'Why are you the last to take steps to bring me back to my house?" Seeing I know everything everyone is saying about my house. You are my brothers, you are my bones and my flesh: so why aren't you taking steps to bring me back? Tell Amasa, aren't you my bone and my flesh? May God do so to me, and more, if I don't make you captain of my armies permanently in place of Joab." The king swayed the heart of the men of Judah, like it was the heart of one man; so they sent word to the king, "You and your servants may return."

The king returned, and went back to Jordan. Everyone in Judah came to Gilgal, to meet the him, and to escort the him over Jordan. Shimei, which was of Bahurim ran down with the men of Judah to meet king David. There were 1,000 men of Benjamin with him, and Ziba, and his fifteen sons and his twenty servants with him; and they went over Jordan before the king. The king's family went over Jordan on a ferry boat, and to do what he thought was good. Shimei fell down before the king, as he was coming over Jordan, and said to the king, "Let not my lord charge me with iniquity, or remember that which your servant did rebelliously the day that my lord the king went out of Jerusalem, that you should take it to heart. Your servant knows that he has sinned: that is why I have come down here before anyone else from Joseph's house to meet you." Abishai answered, "Shouldn't Shimei be put to death for this, for cursing the Lord's anointed?" David said, "What am I going to do with you children of Zeruiah, that you should be enemies of mine? Shall any man be put to death today in Israel? Am I not the king over Israel?" Therefore the king said to Shimei, "I sware to you that you will not die."

Mephibosheth went to meet the king, he had no shoes on his feet, nor had he trimmed his beard, nor did he have clean clothes on from the day that the king left until he came back in peace. When he went to meet the king, the king said to him, "Why didn't you go with me Mephibosheth?" He answered, "My lord, O king, my servant lied to me: for your servant said, I will saddle me a donkey, and ride it and go with the king; because I am lame. He has slandered your servant to my lord the king; but my lord the king is as an angel of God: do whatever you think is best. All of my father's house were but dead men before you: but yet you set me your servant among them at your own table. What right therefore have I yet to complain to you?" The king said to him, "Why are you still talking about all this? I have said, you and Ziba divide the land." Mephibosheth said to the king, "Yes, let him take all of it, forasmuch as my lord the king is come home again in peace."

Barzillai came from Rogelim, and escorted the king over the Jordan. Barzillai was a very old man. He had provided the king with everything he needed while he was at Mahanaim; because he was very wealthy. The king said, "Come with me and I will provide for you while we are in Jerusalem." Barzillai said, "How long is my life going to be, that I should go with you to Jerusalem? I am now 80 years old: do I know good from evil? Can I taste what I eat or what I drink? Can I hear the voices of men and women singing? That is why your servant would only be a burden to you, O king. Your servant will go a little way over Jordan with you and: why should the king repay me with such a reward? Let me, I ask of you, turn and go back, so that I may die in my hometown, and be buried beside my father and mother. Here is your servant Chimham; let him go over Jordan with you, and do to him whatever seems good to you." The king answered, "Chimham will go with me, and I will do for him what seems good to you. Whatever you request of me, that is what I'll do for you."

All the people went across Jordan. When the king was come over, he kissed Barzillai, and blessed him; and he returned to his home.

Afterwards, the king went on to Gilgal, Chimham; all the people of Judah, and half of the people of Israel escorted the king. All of the men of Israel went to the king and said, "Why has our brothers the men of Judah stolen you away, and brought you and your household, and all of your men over Jordan?" The men of Judah answered, "The king is a close relative of ours: why then are you angry about this? Have we eaten at the king's expense, or has he given us any gift?" The men of Israel answered, "We have ten shares in the king, and we also have more right to David than you do. Why then do you despise us, were we not the first to advise bringing back our king?" What the men of Judah said was more harsh than what the men of Israel had said.

There happened to be a rebel there, whose name was Sheba: and he blew a trumpet, and said, "We want nothing to do with David, nor do we want anything he's got, every man to his tents!" Every man left David, and followed Sheba, but the people of Judah stuck by their king from Jordan all the way to Jerusalem. When David returned to his home in Jerusalem; he took his ten concubines, whom he had left there to take care of this home, and put them in seclusion, and fed them, but he did not sleep with one of them. They were in seclusion until their death, living like widows. The king said to Amasa, "Bring me all the men of Judah within the next three days, and make sure you come too." Amasa went to gather all the men of Judah: but he took longer than three days. David said to Abishai, "It looks as if Sheba will do more harm to us than Absalom: take your lord's servants, and go look for him, so he won't be able to build a defense around himself, and escape from us." Abishai, Joab's men, the Cherethites, the Pelethites, and all the mighty men went out looking for Sheba.

When they were at the large stone which is in Gibeon, Amasa came to them. Joab was dressed in battle armor; on it was a belt with a sword fastened in it's sheath at his hips; and as he was going forward, it fell out. Joab said to Amasa, "Do you feel alright, my brother?" Joab grabbed him by the beard with his right hand to kiss him, but Amasa did not pay any attention to the sword that was in Joab's hand; so he struck him with it in the stomach, and his guts fell to the ground, so he did not strike him again, and he died. Joab and Abishai his brother kept on looking for Sheba. One of Joab's soldiers stood beside him, and said, "Whoever favors Joab, and whoever is for David, let him go after Joab." Amasa laid in his own blood on the highway, and when the man saw that everyone was standing still, he took Amasa out of the highway to a field, and laid a cloth on him, when he saw that everyone that came by stopped. When he was out of the highway all the people followed after Joab in search of Sheba.

He went through all the tribes of Israel to Abel, to Beth-maachah, and all the Berites: and they all gathered together, and they all went after Sheba. They came and captured him in Abel of Beth-maachah, and they built a mound against the city; it was by the rampart, and all the people that were with Joab beat on the wall to break it down. A wise woman cried out in the city, "Hear,

hear; what I say, I ask of you Joab, come over here, so that I can speak with you." When he had done so, the woman said, "Are you Joab?" He answered, "I am he." She said, "Listen to the words of your handmaid." He answered, "I will listen." She said, "They used to talk in former times saying, "They shall surely seek guidance at Abel so the arguing would stop. I am among the peaceable and faithful in Israel: you want to destroy a city and a mother in Israel: why do you want to swallow up the inheritance of the Lord?" Joab answered her, "Far be it, far be it from me, that I would swallow up or destroy. "You have misunderstood: it is a man of mount Ephraim, Sheba has lifted up his hand against the king, against David: deliver him only, and I will leave this city." The woman said, "OK, his head shall be thrown over the wall to you." The woman then went to all the people in the city with the information she had. They cut off Sheba's beard and threw it over the wall to Joab. He blew a trumpet, and they left the city, every man went to his tent. Joab returned to Jerusalem to the king.

Joab was the leader of the men of Israel; Benaiah was over the Cherethites and the Pelethites; Adoram was over the tribute: Jehoshaphat was recorder; Sheva was scribe; Zadok and Abiathar were the priests: and Ira was David's priest.

There was a famine during David's reign, three years, consecutive years: and he prayed to the Lord about it. The Lord answered, "It is because of Saul and his bloodthirsty house, because he killed the Gibeonites." Therefore the king sent for the Gibeonites, and said to them; (the Gibeonites were not a part of the children of Israel, but of the Amorites; and the children of Israel had promised to protect them: and Saul tried to kill them in his zeal to the children of Israel and Judah.) "What shall I do for you?" "With what shall I make the atonement, that you may bless the inheritance of the Lord?" The Gibeonites said, "We do not want any silver or gold of Saul's nor anything that's in his house; neither do we want any Israelite to die for us." David said, "Whatever you want me to do, that is what I'll do." They answered, "The man that consumed us, and plotted against us that we should be destroyed from remaining in any of the territories of Israel allow seven of his children be given to us, and we will hang them up unto the Lord in Gibeah of Saul, whom the Lord chose." The king said, "I will give them to you."

The king spared Mephibosheth, because of the Lord's oath that was between him and Jonathan. The king took the two sons of Rizpah the daughter of Aiah, whom Saul fathered, Armoni and Mephibosheth; and the five sons of Michal the daughter of Saul, whom she bore for Adriel. The king gave them to the Gibeonites, and they hung them on the hill before the Lord: and they fell all seven of them at the same time, and were put to death in the days of harvest, in the first days, in the beginning of barley harvest.

Rizpah the daughter of Aiah took sackcloth, and spread it for her upon the rock, from the beginning of harvest until water dropped upon them out of heaven, and did not allow the birds nor any animal to rest on them. Someone told David what Rizpah had done.

David went and took the bones of Saul and of Jonathan his from the men of Jabesh-gilead, which had stolen them from the street of Beth-shan, where the Philistines had hung them, when they had killed Saul in Gilboa: and they gathered the bones of those who had been hung. They buried their bones in the country of Benjamin in Zelah in the tomb of Kish his father: and they performed all that the king commanded. Afterwards God answered their prayer.

The Philistines went to war again with Israel; and David went and his servants with him, and fought against the Philistines: and he grew faint. Ishbi-benob, which was of the sons of the giant (Rapha), whose spear weighed 300 shekels (approx. 11 ¾ pounds) of brass, who had a new sword, thought that he could kill David. Abishai came to help David, and struck the Philistine, and killed him. The men of David swore to him, saying, "You shall go to battle with us any more, that you quench not the light of Israel."

There was again a battle with the Philistines at Gob: then Sibbechai killed Saph, which was one of the children of the giant. There was again a battle with the Philistines in Gob where Elhanan, killed the brother of Goliath, the staff of whose spear was like a weaver's beam. There was again a battle in Gath, where there was a man of great stature, that had six fingers on each hand and six toes on each foot, and he was also the giant's son. When he defied Israel, Jonathan the son of Shammah the brother of David killed him. These four were the children of the giant, and were killed by David and by his servants.

David spoke the words of this song to the Lord, when the Lord had delivered him out of the hand of all his enemies, and out of the hand of Saul. He said, The Lord is my Rock, and my Fortress, and my Deliverer; my God, my Rock; in Him will I trust: He is my Shield and the Horn of my salvation, my High Tower, and my Refuge, my Savior; You save me from violence. I will call on the Lord, Who is worthy to be praised: so shall I be saved from my enemies. When the waves of death surrounded me, the floods of ungodliness scared me. The sorrows of hell surrounded me; the snares of death confronted me. In my distress I called upon the Lord, and cried to my God: and He did hear my voice out of His temple, and my cry did enter into His ears. The earth shook and trembled; the foundations of the heaven moved and shook, because He was angry. There went up a smoke out of His nostrils, and fire out of His mouth devoured: coals were kindled by it. He bowed the heavens also, and came down; and darkness was under His feet. He rode upon a cherub, and did fly: He was seen upon the wings of the wind. He made darkness His canopy around Him, and gathering of waters, and thick clouds of the skies. Through the brightness before Him were coals of fire kindled. The Lord thundered from heaven, and the Most High uttered His voice. He sent out arrows and scattered them: lightning, and vanquished them. The channels of the sea appeared, the foundations of the world were discovered, at the rebuking of the Lord, at the blast of the breath of His nostrils. He sent from above, He took me; He drew me out of many waters. He delivered me from my strong enemy, and from them that hated me: for they were too strong for me. They confronted me in the day of my calamity: but the Lord was my support. He brought me forth also into a large place: He delivered me, because He delighted in me. The Lord rewarded me according to my righteousness; according to the cleanness of my hands has He recompensed me. I have kept the ways of the Lord, and have not wickedly departed from my God. All His judgments were before me: and as for His statutes, I did not depart from them. I was also upright before Him, and have kept myself from my iniquity. Therefore, the Lord has rewarded me according to my righteousness; according to my cleanness in His eyesight. With the merciful You will show Yourself merciful, and with the upright man You will show Yourself upright. With the pure You will show Yourself pure; and with the devious You will show Yourself shrewd. The afflicted people You will save: but Your eyes are upon the proud, that You may bring them down. You are my Lamp, O Lord: and You will lighten my darkness. For by You I can run against a troop: by my God I have leaped over a wall. As for God, His way is perfect; the word of the Lord is proven: He is a shield to all them that trust in Him. For who is God, besides the Lord? Who is a Rock besides our God. God is my strength and power; He makes my way perfect. He makes my feet like that of a deer: and sets me upon my high places. He teaches me to war; so that bronze is bent by my arms. You have also have given me the shield of your salvation: and Your gentleness has made me great. You have enlarged my steps; so that my feet would not slip. I have captured my enemies, and killed them; and did not turn away until they were consumed. I have consumed them, and wounded the, so that they could not arise: they are dead. You have girded me with strength to battle: them that rose up against me You have caused to bow down to me. You have also given me victory over my enemies, so that I could destroy them that hate me. They looked, but there was no one to save them; even unto the Lord, but He answered them not. I beat them as the dust of the earth: I did stamp them as the mire of the street, and did scatter them abroad. You have also delivered me from the contentions of my people, You have kept me to be head of the heathen: a people which I knew not would serve me. Foreigners shall submit themselves unto me: as soon as they hear, they shall be obedient unto me. Foreigners shall fade away, and they shall be afraid in their hideouts. The Lord lives; and blessed be my Rock; and exalted be the God of the Rock of my salvation. It is God that avenges me, and that brings down the people that serve me, and brings me from my enemies: You also have lifted me up on high above them that rose up against me: You have delivered me from that violent man. Therefore I will give thanks to You, O Lord, among that nations, and I will sing praises to Your name. He is the Tower of salvation for His King: and shows mercy to His anointed, unto David, and to his seed for evermore.

These are the last words of David. David, the son of Jesse said, and the man who was raised up on high, the anointed of the God of Jacob, and the sweet psalmist of Israel, said, "The Spirit of the Lord spoke by me, and His Word was what I spoke. The God of Israel said, the

Rock of Israel spoke to me, He that rules over men must be just, ruling in the fear of God. He shall be as the light of the morning, when the sun rises, a morning without clouds; as the tender grass springing out of the earth by clear shining after rain. Although my house is not like this with God: yet He has made with me an everlasting covenant, ordered in al things, and sure: for this is all my salvation, and all my desire, although He will not make it grow. The rebellious ones of Belial shall be as thorns thrust away, because they cannot be captured, but the man that does capture them shall be armored with iron and the staff of a spear; and they shall be utterly burned with fire in the same place.

These are the names of the mighty men whom David had: The Tachmonite, that sat in the seat, chief among the captains; the same was Adino the Eznite: he fought against 800, whom he killed at one time. After him was Eleazar the son of Dodo the Ahohite, one of the three mighty men with David, when they defied the Philistines that were there gathered together for battle, and the men of Israel were gone away: He arose and attacked the Philistines until his hand was weary, and his hand stuck to the sword: and the Lord brought a great victory that day; and the people returned home with him to take the spoil. After him was Shammah the son of Agee the Hararite. The Philistines were gathered together in a troop, where there was some land full of lentils: and everyone ran away from the Philistines, but he stood in the middle of the ground, and defended it, and defeated the Philistines: and the Lord brought a great victory. Three of the thirty top ranked men went to David at harvest time to the cave of Adullam: and the troop of the Philistines camped in the Valley of Rephaim. David was in the stronghold, and the garrison of the Philistines was then in Beth lehem. He said, "Oh that someone would give me a drink of water from the well of Beth-lehem, which is by the gate!" The three mighty men broke through the army of the Philistines, and drew water out of the well of Beth-lehem, that was by the gate, and took it, and brought it to David: but he would not drink it, but poured it out unto the Lord, and he said, "Be it far from me, O Lord, that I should do this: is not this the blood of the men that went in jeopardy of their lives?" Therefore he would not drink it. These things did these three mighty men.

And Abishai, the brother of Joab, the son of Zeruiah, was chief among another three. And he killed three-hundred men with his spear, and won a name among these three. Was he not the most honorable of the three? Therefore he was their captain: but he would not count himself with the first three.

Benaiah, who had done many deeds, he killed two loin-like men of Moab: he also killed a lion in a pit in the snow: he killed an Egyptian, a spectacular man, the Egyptian had a spear in his hand; but he went down on him with a staff, took the spear away from the Egyptian, and killed him with it. These are the things that Benaiah did, and he had the most honorable name among three mighty men. He was more honorable than the thirty, but he would not count himself with the first three. And David appointed him over his guard.

Asahel was one of the thirty; Elhanan, Shammah, Elika, Helez, Ira, Abiezer, Mebunnai, Zalmon, Maharai, Heleb, Ittai,Benaiah, Hiddai, Abi-albon, Azmaveth, Eliahba, Jonathan, Shammah, Ahiam, Eliphelet,, Eliam, Hezrai, Paarai, Igai, Bani, Zelek, Naharai, the armor-bearer to Joab Ira, Gareb, Uriah the: thirty-seven in all.

Again the Lord was angry with Israel and He moved David against them to say, "Go, take a census of Israel and Judah." The king said to Joab the captain of the army, which was with him, "Go through all of the tribes of Israel, from Dan to Beer-sheba, and count the people, so that I will know how many of them there are." Joab said, "Now may the Lord your God add to the people a hundred times more than there are, and may my lord the king see it; but why does my lord the king want to do this?" Nevertheless, the king's word overruled Joab's, and also the captains of the armies. Joab and the captains of the armies left the king to take a census of Israel. They went through Jordan, and camped in Aroer, on the right side of the city that lies in the middle of the ravine of Gad, and toward Jazer: then they went to Gilead, and to the land of Tahtim-hodshi; and they went to Dan-jaan, and to Zidon; then to the fortress of Tyre, and to all the cities of the Hivites, and of the Canaanites: and they went out to the south of Judah, to Beer sheba. When they had gone through all the land, they came to Jerusalem, nine months and twenty days later. Joab gave the total count of the people to the king: and there were in Israel 800,000 valiant men that would fight; and 500,000 men of Judah. (1,300,000 total)

David's conscience bothered him after that he had taken the census. He said to the Lord, "I have sinned greatly in what I have done: and now, I ask You, O Lord, take away the iniquity of Your servant; for my foolish action." When David arose the next morning, the word of the Lord came to the prophet Gad, David's seer, saying, "Go and say to David, "This is what the Lord says, I offer you three things; choose one of them, that I may do it unto you." Therefore Gad went to David, and told him, "Shall seven year of famine come to you in your land?; or will you flee three months before your pursuing enemies?; or do you prefer three days of pestilence (plague) in your land. Tell me now, and I will tell the One who sent me." David said, I am in great distress: Let us fall into the Lord's hands; because His mercies are great: and don't let me fall into the hands of man." Therefore, the Lord allowed a plague to come upon Israel for three days: and 70,000 men died in Israel. When the angel stretched out His hand over Jerusalem to destroy it, the Lord would not allow it's destruction. The Lord said to the angel that killed the people, "That's enough: restrain your hand." The angel of the Lord was by the threshing place of Araunah.

David spoke to the Lord when he saw the angel that killed the people, and said, "Surely I have sinned, and I have done wickedly: but these sheep, what have they done? Let your hand, I ask, be against me, and against my father's house." Gad went to David that day, and said to him, "Go up, and build an altar unto the Lord in the threshing floor of Araunah." David did exactly what the Lord had commanded him to do. Araunah looked, and saw the king and his servants coming toward him: and he went out, and bowed down before the king with his face to the ground; and said, "Why has my lord the king come to his servant?" David said, "To buy the threshing floor from you, to build an altar unto the Lord, so that the plague may be taken away from the people." Araunah said, "You can take and offer up what your think is best: there is oxen for burnt sacrifice, and threshing instruments and instruments of the oxen for wood. All these, O king, I will give to you. "May the Lord thy God accept you." The king said, "No; but

I will by it from you at a price: neither will I offer burnt offerings unto the Lord my God from that which costs me nothing." Therefore, David bought the threshing floor and the oxen for fifty shekels of silver. ($6,400) He built there an altar unto the Lord, and offered burnt offerings and peace offerings. The Lord answered David's prayer and the plague was lifted from Israel.

King David was was about 70 years old, and they covered him with clothes, but he could not get warm. His servants said to him, "Let us go find a young woman for my lord the king and let her serve you, and care for you, and let her lay beside you so you can get warm." They looked for a pretty woman throughout all the coasts of Israel, and found Abishag a Shunammite, and brought her to the king. She took care of the king; but the he could not make love to her.

Pride filled Adonijah's heart (David's forth son) and he said, "I will reign as king." He prepared for himself chariots, horsemen, and fifty men to run before him. His father had never said, "Why have you done this?" He also was a very good-looking man. He talked with Joab, and with Abiathar the priest, and they followed Adonijah and helped him. Zadok the other priest, Benaiah, Nathan the prophet, Shimei, Rei, and the mighty men which belonged to David, were not with Adonijah.

Adonijah killed sheep, oxen and fat cattle by the stone of Zoheleth, which is by Enrogel, and gathered together all his brothers, and all the men of Judah the king's servants; but Nathan the prophet, Benaiah, the mighty men, and Solomon his brother, he did not ask to be there. Meanwhile Nathan spoke to Bath-sheba, Solomon's mother and said, "Have your not heard that Adonijah, has become king, and David our lord doesn't know. Now therefore let me tell you what to do, so that you will save your life and Solomon's. Go to king David, and say to him, Didn't you, my lord, O king, promise your handmaiden, saying for sure Solomon your son shall reign after me, and he shall sit upon my throne? Why then is Adonijah king? While you are talking with the him, I will come in after you, and agree with what you have said." Bath-sheba went to the king's chamber, and the king was very old; Abishag took care of him. Bath-sheba bowed down to give honor to the king, and the king said, "What is your wish?" She said, "My lord, you swore by the Lord thy God to me, that Solomon, my son, would reign after you, and that he would sit upon your throne. Now, Adoijah reigns, and you know nothing about it. He has killed many of the oxen, fat cattle and sheep, and has gathered together all of your sons, Abiathar the priest, and Joab the captain of the armies: but Solomon your servant is not there. You my lord, O king, everyone is Israel is waiting to see what you will tell them, who shall sit on the throne of my lord the king. Otherwise, this will happen, when my lord the king shall die like his fathers, that I and my son Solomon shall be counted as offenders." While she was talking with the king, Nathan the prophet walked in. She told the king, "Here is Nathan the prophet." When he came in the room he bowed down before the king with his face toward the ground. Nathan said, "My lord, O king, have you said that Adonijah will reign after you, that he should sit upon your throne? He has went and killed a lot of oxen, fat cattle and sheep and has gathered together all of your sons, the captains of the armies, and Abiathar the priest; and they eat and drink with him, and say, Long live king Adonijah; but me, your servant, Zadok the priest, Benaiah, and your son Solomon, he doesn't want there. Did you do this, my lord the king? Why haven't you told your servant, who should sit on the throne of my lord the king after him?" King David answered and said, "Bring Bath-sheba back in here." She came in the room and stood before the king. The king swore to her, "As the Lord lives, that has redeemed my soul out of all distress, I sware to you by the Lord God of Israel, Solomon your son will definitely reign after me, and he shall sit upon my throne in my place; I will certainly do this today." Bath-sheba bowed with her face to the earth, and reverenced the king, and said, "Let my lord king David live for ever." He said, "Bring Zadok the priest, Nathan the prophet, and Benaiah in here." They went into the king's chambers; and the king said to them, "Take my servants, and make Solomon my son ride on my mule, to Gihon: and let Zadok the priest and Nathan the prophet anoint him king over Israel: and blow a trumpet, and say, Long live king Solomon. Follow him back, and he shall sit upon my throne: he shall be king in my place: I have appointed him to be ruler over Israel and Judah." Benaiah said, "Amen: the Lord God of my lord the king says so too, as the Lord has been with my lord the king, so shall He also be with Solomon, and make his throne greater than the throne of my lord king David."

Therefore, Zadok the priest, Nathan the prophet, Benaiah, the Cherethites, and the Pelethites went and made Solomon ride upon king David's mule, and took him to Gihon.

Zadok the priest took a horn of oil out of the tabernacle, and anointed Solomon. They blew a trumpet; and all of the people said, "Long live king Solomon." They all followed him, played their flutes, and rejoiced with great joy, and the earth resounded with the joyful sound.

Adonijah and all the people that where with him heard it as they were finishing their meal. When Joab heard the sound of the trumpet, he said, "What is the noise in the city causing such an uproar?" While he was talking, Jonathan the son of Abiathar the priest came in; and Adonijah said to him, "Come in; because you are a trustworthy man, and bring good news." Jonathan answered and said, "Without a doubt our lord king David has made Solomon king. The king has sent with him Zadok the priest, Nathan the prophet, Beaiah, the Cherethites, and the Pelethites, and they have made him ride upon the king's mule: Zadok the priest, and Nathan the prophet have anointed him king in Gihon: and they have come back here rejoicing, so that the city resounds. This is the sound you have heard. Solomon sits on the throne of the kingdom." When the king's servants came to bless our lord king David, saying, May God make Solomon's name better than your name, and make his throne greater than your throne. The king bowed down on the bed; and he said, Blessed be the Lord God of Israel, which has given one to sit on my throne today, and allowing me to see it." All the people that were with Adonijah were afraid, and got up and went on their way.

Adonijah was afraid of Solomon, and left and went and grabbed hold of the horns of the altar. Someone told Solomon that Adonijah was afraid of him; because he has grabbed hold of the horns of the altar, and said, "Let king Solomon swear to me today that he will not kill his servant with a sword." Solomon said, "If he will prove that he is a worthy man, there will not be a hair of his fall to the ground; but if wickedness be found in him, he will die." Therefore king Solomon sent for him, and they brought him from the altar. He went and bowed down before the king, and Solomon said to him, "Go home."

The end of David's life drew near; and he commanded Solomon his son, saying, "I go the way of all the earth: be strong and show yourself a man; and keep the commandments of the Lord thy God, to walk in His ways, to keep His statutes, His commandments, His judgments, and His testimonies, as it is written in the law of Moses, that you may prosper in all that you do, and wherever you turn: that the Lord may continue His word which he spoke concerning me, saying, "If your children take heed to their way, to walk before Me in truth with all their heart and with all their soul, there shall not fail thee (said He) a man on the throne of Israel."

You also know what Joab did to me, and what he did to the two captains of the armies of Israel, to Abner, and Amasa, whom he killed, and shed the blood of war in peace, and put the blood of war upon his clothes that he was wearing, and in his shoes that were on his feet. Use wisdom and do to him what you think is right, and let not his gray hair go down to the grave in peace, but be kind to the sons of Barzillai, and let them eat at your table: because they helped me when ran away because of your brother. You have with you Shimei, which cursed me with a grievous curse when I went to Mahanaim: but he came down to meet me at Jordan, and I swore to him by the Lord, that I would not kill him with a sword. Don't count him as guiltless: for you are a wise man, and you know what you should do to him; but his gray hair take to the grave with blood."

David died and joined his ancestors, and was buried in the city of David. He reigned over Israel 40 years: 7 years in Hebron, and 33 years in Jerusalem.

Solomon, then sat upon the throne of David his father; and his kingdom was firmly established.

THE DAVIDIC COVENANT

The story of King David is an awesome story of how God took a young shepherd boy and turned him into a king. After Saul had failed as king over God's people, God found a "man after His own heart." (I Samuel 13:14) David lived an exciting life to say the least, but even though he made his share of mistakes his first priority was pleasing God.

The Covenant

Out of David's love and zeal for God, he wanted to build a house for the Ark of God, but God had something else in mind; He wanted to build a David a house, not a temporal one, but an everlasting one. After clear direction from God, Nathan the prophet told David, "When thy days be fulfilled, and thou shalt sleep with thy fathers, I will set up thy seed after thee, which shall proceed out of thy bowels, and I will establish his kingdom.

He shall build a house for My name, and I will stablish the throne of his kingdom forever. I will be his Father, and he shall be My son. If he commit iniquity, I will chasten him with the rod of men, and with the stripes of the children of men: But My mercy shall not depart away from him, as I took it from Saul, whom I put away before thee. And thine house and thy kingdom shall be established for ever before thee: thy throne shall be established for ever. (2 Samuel 7:12-16)

And again God establishes His covenant with David. "My mercy will I keep for him for evermore, and My covenant shall stand fast with him. His seed also will I make to endure for ever, and his throne as the days of heaven. Ifhis children forsake my law, and walk not in My judgments; If they break My statutes, and keep not My commandments; Then will I visit their transgression with the rod, and their iniquity with stripes. Nevertheless My loving-kindness will I not utterly take from him, nor suffer My faithfulness to fail. My covenant will I not break nor alter the thing that is gone out of My lips. Once have I sworn by My holiness that I will not lie unto David. His seed shall endure forever, and his throne as the sun before Me. It shall be established for ever as the moon, and as the faithful witness in heaven." (Psalm 89:28-37)

The Fulfillment

How does God plan on fulfilling the covenant that He made with David? Thru His Son!!!

"Behold, the days come", saith the Lord, "that I will raise unto David a righteous Branch, and a King shall reign and prosper, and shall execute judgment and justice in the earth. In His days Judah shall be saved, and Israel shall dwell safely: and this is His name whereby He shall be called, THE LORD OUR RIGHTEOUSNESS." (Jeremiah 23:5-6)

And the seventh angel sounded; and there were great voices in heaven, saying, THE KINGOMS OF THIS WORLD ARE BECOME THE KINGDOMS OF OUR LORD, AND OF HIS CHRIST, AND HE SHALL REIGN FOR EVER AND EVER. (Revelation 11:15)

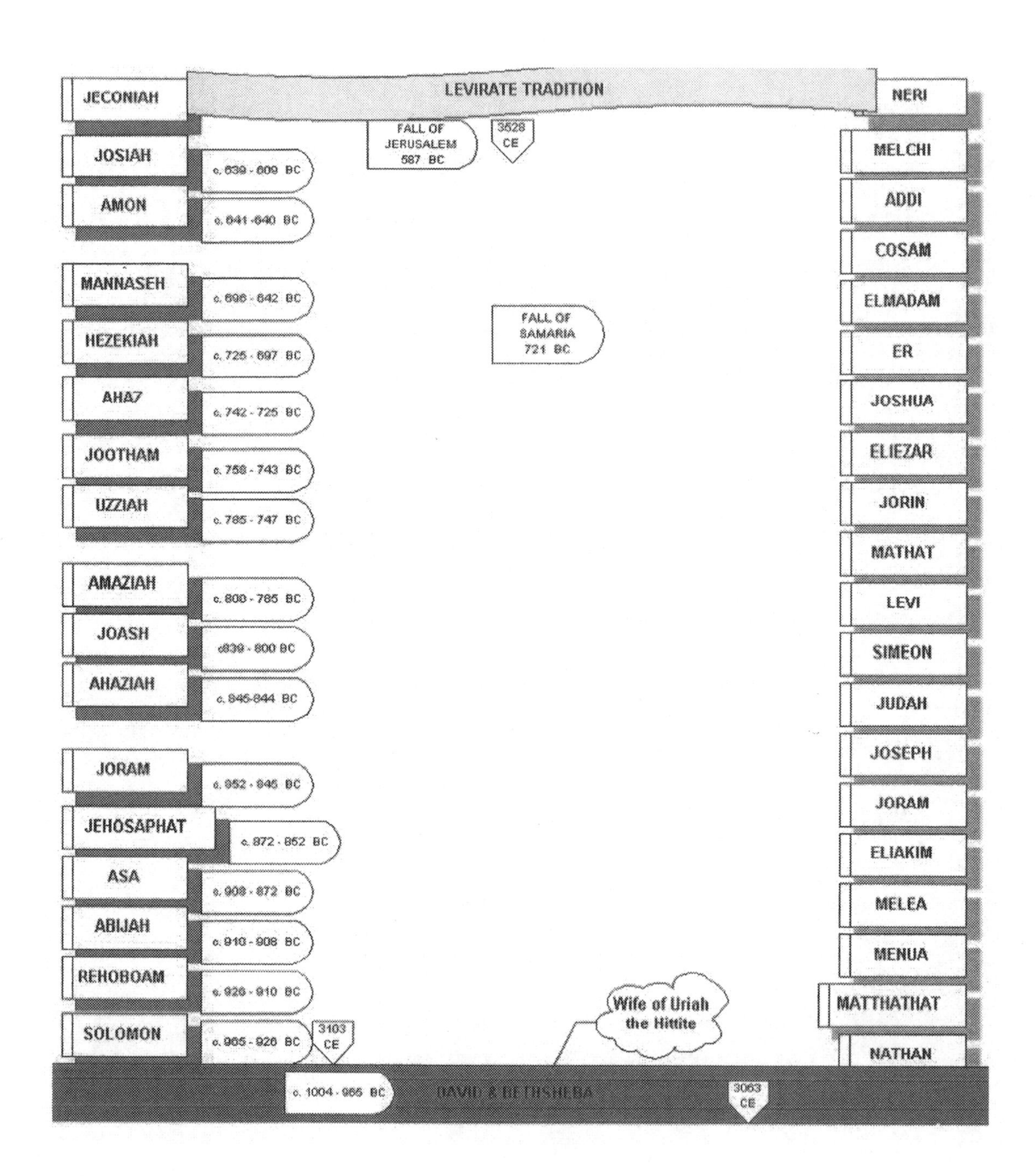
LEVIRATE TRADITION
JECONIAH
NERI
FALL OF
JERUSALEM
587 BC
3528
CE
JOSIAH
c. 639 - 609 BC
AMON
c. 641 -640 BC
MANNASEH
c. 696 - 642 BC
HEZEKIAH
c. 725 - 697 BC
AHAZ
c. 742 - 725 BC
JOOTHAM
c. 758 - 743 BC
UZZIAH
c. 785 - 747 BC
AMAZIAH
c. 800 - 785 BC
JOASH
c839 - 800 BC
AHAZIAH
c. 846-844 BC
JORAM
c. 852 - 846 BC
JEHOSAPHAT
c. 872 - 852 BC
ASA
c. 908 - 872 BC
ABIJAH
c. 910 - 908 BC
REHOBOAM
c. 926 - 910 BC
SOLOMON
c. 965 - 926 BC
3103
CE
FALL OF
SAMARIA
721 BC
MELCHI
ADDI
COSAM
ELMADAM
ER
JOSHUA
ELIEZAR
JORIN
MATHAT
LEVI
SIMEON
JUDAH
JOSEPH
JORAM
ELIAKIM
MELEA
MENUA
MATTHATHAT
NATHAN
Wife of Uriah
the Hittite
c. 1004 - 965 BC
DAVID & BETHSHEBA
3063
CE

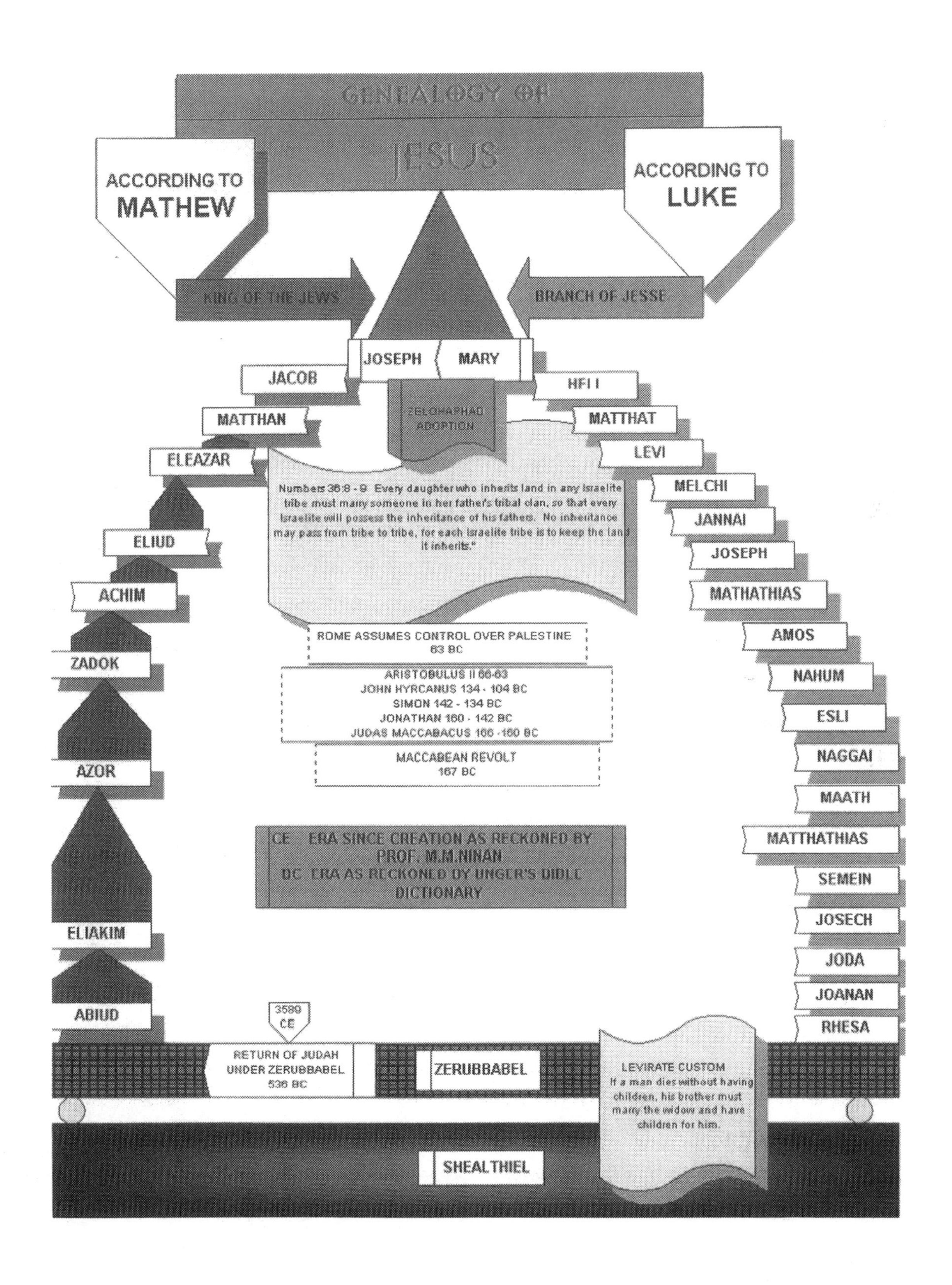
GENEALOGY OF
JESUS
ACCORDING TO
MATHEW
ACCORDING TO
LUKE
KING OF THE JEWS
BRANCH OF JESSE
JOSEPH
MARY
ZELOHAPHAD
ADOPTION
JACOB
MATTHAN
ELEAZAR
ELIUD
ACHIM
ZADOK
AZOR
ELIAKIM
ABIUD
HFI I
MATTHAT
LEVI
MELCHI
JANNAI
JOSEPH
MATHATHIAS
AMOS
NAHUM
ESLI
NAGGAI
MAATH
MATTHATHIAS
SEMEIN
JOSECH
JODA
JOANAN
RHESA
Numbers 36:8 - 9 Every daughter who inherits land in any Israelite tribe must marry someone in her father's tribal clan, so that every Israelite will possess the inheritance of his fathers. No inheritance may pass from tribe to tribe, for each Israelite tribe is to keep the land it inherits."
ROME ASSUMES CONTROL OVER PALESTINE
63 BC
ARISTOBULUS II 66-63
JOHN HYRCANUS 134 - 104 BC
SIMON 142 - 134 BC
JONATHAN 160 - 142 BC
JUDAS MACCABACUS 166 -160 BC
MACCABEAN REVOLT
167 BC
CE ERA SINCE CREATION AS RECKONED BY
PROF. M.M.NINAN
BC ERA AS RECKONED BY UNGER'S BIBLE
DICTIONARY
3589
CE
RETURN OF JUDAH
UNDER ZERUBBABEL
536 BC
ZERUBBABEL
LEVIRATE CUSTOM
If a man dies without having children, his brother must marry the widow and have children for him.
SHEALTHIEL